sew zoey

SWATCH OUT!

written by
Chloe Taylor

illustrated by
Nancy Zhang

Simon Spotlight

New York London Toronto Sydney New Delhi

SIMON SPOTLIGHT
An imprint of Simon & Schuster Children's Publishing Division
1230 Avenue of the Americas, New York, New York 10020
Copyright © 2014 by Simon & Schuster, Inc.
All rights reserved, including the right of reproduction in whole or
in part in any form.
SIMON SPOTLIGHT and colophon are registered trademarks of
Simon & Schuster, Inc.
Text by Caroline Hickey
Designed by Laura Roode
For information about special discounts for bulk purchases, please contact
Simon & Schuster Special Sales at 1-866-506-1949 or
business@simonandschuster.com.
Manufactured in the United States of America 0514 FFG
First Edition 10 9 8 7 6 5 4 3 2 1
ISBN 978-1-4814-1535-4 (pb)
ISBN 978-1-4814-1536-1 (hc)
ISBN 978-1-4814-1537-8 (eBook)
The Library of Congress has catalogued this title.

----- CHAPTER 1 -----

It's a Mystery!

You have NO idea how excited I am to be blogging again! After six weeks away at camp, being able to just pick up my laptop and blog whenever I want to feels AMAZING!

School's starting pretty soon, but there's enough

summer left for a few small adventures, right? And even though my top priority is to be a good friend to one of my besties who really needs me at the moment, I've also got a mystery to solve. A *fashion* mystery. That's right! I *think* I've figured out the identity of my longtime "mysterious benefactor," Fashionsista. I'm still not sure how I feel about finding out for SURE who she is. After all, there's something pretty awesome about having a secret friend who sends you amazing gifts! But I think it's time. So, Fashionsista, if you're reading this, check your mailbox for a letter from me. I'll be mailing it to you just as soon as I get the courage to put it in the mailbox. . . . At least, I think it'll be to you!

And in honor of the potential unmasking of my secret friend, I've posted a sketch of a masquerade outfit. . . . Isn't it dramatic? Probably too much for the first day of school, though, right?

Zoey Webber was having a blast. It had been way too long since she'd spent a lazy afternoon at the community pool with friends, and she'd even been lucky enough to get a ride there from her older brother, Marcus, who was working as a lifeguard for the summer.

Zoey and her friends Priti Holbrooke and Libby Flynn had found three lounge chairs near the diving well, and they were stretched out chatting. Libby was filling Priti and Zoey in on the details of her ballet camp after Priti and Zoey shared stories from their six weeks at sleepaway camp. The only thing that could have made the afternoon better was if their other friend, Kate Mackey, could have been there too. But she was at preseason swim camp for another week.

"Guys, I have to tell you something," Zoey whispered. The girls leaned in closer, sensing a secret coming. "My brother is *seriously* losing it."

Priti and Libby both swiveled their eyes toward Marcus, who was perched on the lifeguard stand by the lap lanes. He wore sunglasses and a visor, and he appeared to be watching some young kids in the shallow end.

Priti squinted. "He looks fine to me, Zoey. What do you mean?"

Zoey blew out a breath that made her bangs fly

up in the air. "I mean, he's in total *la-la land* over my friend Allie. They've been dating all summer, and he's completely spacey all the time! I asked him to put my pool bag in the car this morning, when we were leaving, and instead of putting it in the car, he put it back up in my *room*. I was in the kitchen, so I didn't notice, and then halfway to the pool I realized it wasn't in the backseat! So now I don't have clothes to wear to meet Kate for ice cream later."

"Ah-HA! So *that's* why you texted me to bring an extra towel." Priti laughed loudly. "I figured you'd been sketching and just forgot to pack your stuff."

Zoey laughed too. "Well, I'm not saying that would never happen, but it didn't today. Allie called him right as we were leaving, and he got all distracted. And he's making my dad nuts because he's always texting with Allie during dinner."

"My parents *hate* that," Libby said. "I have to leave my phone up in my room during dinner. They like meals to be for family conversation only."

At the word "family," Zoey noticed a shadow cross Priti's face. Priti's parents had just recently decided to divorce, and Zoey knew how hard Priti was taking it.

"You okay, Priti?" Zoey asked. Priti was normally the life of any party, louder and more cheerful and zanier than anyone else. But since she'd gotten the news from her parents, she'd been subdued.

Priti nodded, but her shoulders wiggled up and down too, so it was more of a shrug than a nod, and seemed to mean, *Sorta, but not really.*

"It's just so weird," Priti said. "I came home from camp, and my dad moved out, and now it's just me and Mom and my sisters at home. It was so fast! Like, blink—no more Dad."

Priti was sitting in the middle of the three girls, and without a word, Libby and Zoey leaned toward her and squashed her with a hug. It was a Priti sandwich, and after a few seconds, Priti had to burst out laughing.

Zoey pulled back and smiled. "We knew that was in there somewhere! Should we sandwich you again?"

Priti held up a hand. "No, please! Just change the subject. I'm fine as long as you guys keep talking." She turned to Libby and patted her leg. "What's new with you, Libs? Tell me everything. Pirouettes, pliés?"

Libby—who was normally the sweet, easygoing one—surprised the girls by saying, "Well, actually, my little sister is driving me bonkers."

"You mean Sophie?" Zoey cocked her head, curiously. Sophie was little, only about six years old, and the girls hardly ever saw her. With the age difference, and Sophie still being in elementary school, their schedules just didn't intersect.

Libby nodded guiltily. "I feel terrible even saying it. But Sophie's really sensitive—like me, but even more so—and she cries all the time. I try to be understanding and help her, but she gets upset about literally *everything*. And we've been home together so much this summer!"

Priti grabbed Libby's hand sympathetically. "Just because you're sisters doesn't mean you have to like each other all the time! My older sisters drive me bonkers, too, and they're way past the crying phase. I think that's just how siblings are."

Zoey wanted to chime in too, but Marcus didn't

really drive Zoey bonkers. He was a pretty great brother, actually. Although he *had* been pretty dopey for putting her pool bag back up in her room. But since he'd also given her a ride, and had been nice enough to agree to take her to meet Kate later, she decided it was a draw. He was still a good brother.

Libby sighed. "I know this sounds crazy, but I'm pretty excited for school to start in a few weeks, so I won't be home as much. Even homework seems better than calming Sophie down from yet another tantrum!"

The girls laughed, and Priti nodded. "I'm ready for school too. I need to get out of my house and stop thinking about my family problems!"

"Do you know what *I'm* looking forward to?" Zoey added. "Tomorrow night's Cody Calloway concert!"

She and Libby clutched hands and then squealed. Several people sitting nearby turned to stare at them, and Zoey blushed. She hadn't meant to sound like the crazy tween fan of a gorgeous teen heartthrob, but that's exactly what she was. Cody Calloway *was* gorgeous and had an awesome new album out, and best of all, Libby's mom was taking her, Libby, and Sophie to his concert. Zoey would actually *be* in the same venue as Cody. She desperately needed the right outfit!

Priti smiled and shook her head. "Cody's all right, but, really, he's not *nearly* as cute as Joey Joseph-Brown."

Priti always said that, so Zoey took it in stride. She'd let Priti have her opinion, even though it was wrong—Cody was the best-looking boy on the planet. Zoey had even put a picture of him on the back of her bedroom door, so she could see him whenever her door was closed.

The girls enjoyed the sunshine and talked awhile more, until Marcus's shift was over and he came to collect Zoey. Libby and Priti planned to stay until Libby's mother came to get them after work.

Priti very nicely loaned Zoey a long T-shirt to wear to the ice cream parlor, so she wouldn't have to go in just her bathing suit. It wasn't exactly the outfit Zoey would have chosen, but at least it wasn't a Joey Joseph-Brown T-shirt. That would make her feel like a traitor.

As they drove to the ice cream parlor, Marcus said, "By the way, Allie's coming too."

"Of course," Zoey teased good-naturedly. "I'd hate for you guys to spend a single *minute* apart."

"Ha-ha," Marcus said. "You're hilarious."

"No, you are."

"No, *you* are."

The teasing continued until they arrived at the parlor, and Zoey saw her oldest friend in the world, Kate Mackey, waiting for her. Kate was fresh from swim camp and looked as damp and messy as Zoey.

The girls hugged and then went straight to the counter to order. Mrs. Simms, the owner, happened to be wearing the cloth headband, in the store's colors, that Zoey had made for her several months before. It always gave Zoey a thrill to see someone wearing one of her designs. It made her feel like she was really on her way to being a top designer one day.

Allie came through the doorway a few minutes later and zoomed toward Marcus. After they'd said hello, she came over to Zoey and Kate, who'd already ordered.

"Hi, Zoey!" said Allie, giving her a hug. "You're back from camp! How was it?"

"Good," Zoey replied. "I had a blast. But I definitely missed blogging and my friends from home! How's your summer been?"

Allie smiled shyly, edging closer to Marcus. "Pretty awesome. I added some new accessories to my Etsy site, and I'm superbusy with orders."

"That's great!" Zoey said. "I'll check it out."

There weren't any tables for four available in the ice cream parlor, so Kate and Zoey grabbed a high table for two by the windows, and Allie and Marcus sat in the back.

Once they were seated, Kate and Zoey couldn't help sneaking peeks at Allie and Marcus sitting close together, their heads nearly touching as they shared a hot fudge sundae.

Kate giggled. "Wow. They are in loooove."

It wasn't the type of thing Kate usually noticed or cared about, which made the observation doubly funny to Zoey. "They are. Loooove for sure."

Kate started to lick her double scoop of praline delight, but she stopped and said, "Oh my gosh!

I was so distracted by watching Marcus and Allie that I forgot to tell you the news! I was voted swim team captain today!"

Zoey nearly dropped her own cone. Not that it was such a surprise—after all, Kate was an amazing swimmer and always did her best to support her teammates—but it was surprising that Kate hadn't told her the moment they'd arrived.

"That's *so* awesome!" Zoey said. "You deserve it. You'll be the best captain ever! Ice cream toast!"

The girls giggled and clinked their cones together. Some praline delight glommed on to Zoey's triple fudge, but she didn't mind.

"I have something to tell you, too," Zoey said, leaning close, as if she might be overheard. "I finally wrote a letter to Daphne Shaw, asking if she was Fashionsista. It took me, like, an hour, and the letter is only half a page long! But I'm too scared to send it. I mean, what if it *is* Daphne, but she doesn't want to be unmasked? Or worse, what if it *isn't*, and she thinks I'm a crazy stalker-fan? I just don't know if I should mail it or not."

Zoey shook her head woefully and then bit

off a huge mouthful of ice cream.

Kate took a few licks of her own cone, looking thoughtful. "Well," she began, "I'll tell you something. When I'm on the field playing soccer, or swimming in a meet, I don't have time to think. I have to just *act*. If someone in the lane next to me is about to pass me, or someone's going to steal my ball, there's no way I can wait to weigh the pros and cons. So I just *do*. I listen to whatever my gut tells me, and I go for it."

Zoey listened, nodding her head slightly. Kate made sense. Zoey knew the reason she'd been somewhat successful so far as a designer was because she kept *doing*. She created her blog, and made outfits for friends, and ran her Myfundmaker campaign for Doggie Duds, and started her Etsy store. And she didn't know in advance how any of those ventures would have turned out—she just went for it. So maybe the same was true with Fashionsista's identity.

She just needed to go for it.

Only—and this was where Zoey had to listen to the voice deep down in her belly—what if she didn't *want* to let the mystery go yet? What if the reason she was dragging her feet was to eke out every last bit of suspense?

It was something to think about.

"Great advice," Zoey told Kate. "You really should be team captain."

Kate laughed, blushing slightly at being called a team captain. Then, suddenly, Zoey remembered the other thing she wanted to discuss with Kate: Priti.

"When we were at the pool today, Priti kept talking about her parents," Zoey said. "And she was trying to laugh and be herself, but she seemed overwhelmed. And I have no idea what to say to help her!"

"Me neither," Kate said, licking a drop of ice cream that was pooling on the rim of her cone.

Kate's parents were high school sweethearts, and still very happy together, and Zoey's mother had passed away so long ago that to Zoey, having one parent around the house was totally, 100 percent normal.

"Maybe we should do something to cheer her up," Kate suggested. "Something to take her mind off of it."

Zoey agreed immediately. "How about a day at the beach? We'll get Libby, and the four of us can spend the whole day there—away from everything that's going on at Priti's house."

"Brilliant!" said Kate. "Who doesn't love a day at the beach? Let's do it next week. I'll ask my mom to drive."

Relieved they'd come up with a plan to help their friend, the girls concentrated on finishing their ice cream.

As Kate bit off one of the last remaining chunks of her cone, she said, "Maybe *you* should be team captain of something, Zoey. You've got a lot of team spirit. And you could design yourself a special little captain's hat to wear!"

Both girls laughed until they couldn't laugh anymore.

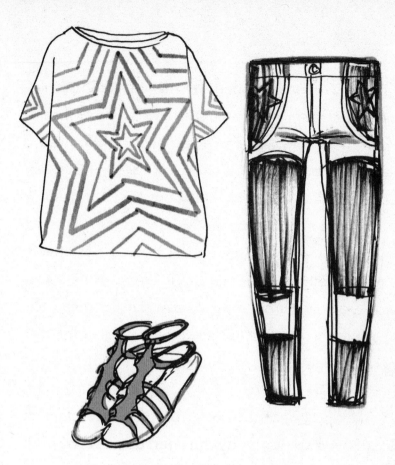

CHAPTER 2

Concert Chic!

In case you don't already know that I love Cody Calloway—I LOVE CODY CALLOWAY! I'm heading off to his concert tonight and I've spent all day working on my outfit. You can see in the sketch that I wanted a rock 'n' roll vibe, but sort of modern rock. That's why

I made the pants cropped, with fake leather details, and paired them with sandals. The vintage rock T-shirt I borrowed from Marcus. (*Shh!* I normally wouldn't borrow without asking, but it looks so great, I couldn't resist!) What do you think? Will Cody love it?

For those of you who are wondering, *no*, I haven't mailed my letter to the person I think is my fashion fairy godmother, Fashionsista, yet. Even despite some excellent advice from my pal Kate! But I'm going to, I'm really going to . . . Just need to scrounge up a little more courage . . .

Zoey paced anxiously by the front door. Libby and her mother and little sister would be arriving any second to take Zoey to the concert. She'd checked her hair and outfit fifteen times to make sure she looked perfect. She had her cell phone, some money, and her concert ticket in her purse. She'd gone to the bathroom. All she needed now was her ride. And for Marcus not to notice she was going out in his T-shirt! Luckily he was upstairs getting ready for his date with Allie, and she'd be gone by the time he came downstairs.

Unfortunately, a second later, Marcus thumped down the stairs and raced by her. He began searching the sofa cushions in the living room and scanning the tops of tables.

"Keys, keys," he muttered. He paused in his search, and his eyes landed on Zoey and her outfit. "Hey, that's my shirt, Zoey. You know you can't borrow my vintage concert shirts!"

"Marcus, *please*," Zoey begged. "This is the most important night of my life! I promise to take good care of it. I'll wash it when I get home."

"Seeing *Cody Calloway* is the most important night of your life?" Marcus guffawed. "The guy probably lipsynchs. And he wears those dopey fedoras. . . ."

"They aren't dopey," Zoey snapped. "They're very hip."

"Where are my *keys*?" Marcus groaned. "I'm supposed to pick up Allie in five minutes, and I don't want to be late."

Zoey suddenly remembered she'd seen his keys while she was getting ready. "I'll tell you where your keys are if I can borrow the shirt."

Marcus narrowed his eyes at her but nodded. "Okay, deal."

Zoey smiled triumphantly as she saw Libby's mom's car pull up out front. "They're upstairs in the bathroom, next to the sink. That's my ride, gotta go!"

Pleased with herself, Zoey bolted out the door, ready for her awesome evening.

The concert arena was packed, mostly with young fans like Zoey, Libby, and Sophie. The girls had good seats—about halfway up and to the left of the stage. While they were waiting for Cody to come on, Mrs. Flynn went to get them all soft pretzels and lemonade.

"Zoey, I'm so glad you came with us!" Sophie said. She had asked to sit next to Zoey and was very nearly in her lap. Libby always said Sophie was shy and didn't talk much, but Zoey had asked Sophie a few questions about her summer in the car, and since then, she hadn't left Zoey's side. "Do you know all of Cody's songs?"

Zoey nodded. "I do. Do you?"

Sophie nodded vigorously. "Yes! I sing them all the time. I'm so excited to be here!"

Libby and Zoey looked at each other and smiled. It was nice to see Sophie be as thrilled as they were.

When Mrs. Flynn returned with the snacks, she handed them out and then sat down. "Zoey, I've been meaning to ask you something. I just took Sophie back-to-school shopping and could hardly find *anything* that fit her properly."

"Really?" Zoey answered, surprised. Sophie was tall and slender, not normally a difficult body type to fit.

Mrs. Flynn sighed. "I'm afraid so. Sophie is tall for her age, like Libby, but when I buy things that are *long* enough for her, they're too *wide*, and she's just swimming in them! I can always get them tailored, of course, and I have some hand-me-downs that were Libby's for her to wear, but I'd love for Sophie to have something really special for her first day of first grade."

Zoey could hear the unasked question in Mrs. Flynn's voice. "Would you like me to make an outfit for her?" she asked.

"Oh, would you?" Mrs. Flynn smiled hopefully, and Sophie looked at Zoey nervously, as if she were asking for a million dollars instead of a simple outfit.

Zoey's face broke into a huge grin. "Of course! I'd be delighted." She wrapped an arm across Sophie's shoulders and pulled her in for a squeeze. "We'll make you something really special, Sophie," she said. "Something you can't find in stores. And you can help me design it!"

Mrs. Flynn clapped her hands together. "Oh, thank you, Zoey! That's so kind of you. Sophie's been wearing dresses so short, they look like tunics, and she ends up having to wear leggings with everything—even when it's warm out!"

"We'll fix that," Zoey assured her. "We should probably get started soon, though, so I have time to finish before school starts. I usually hang out at my aunt Lulu's house when my dad's at work, so maybe you and Sophie could come by this week, so I can measure her and we can talk about ideas?"

"Yes!" yelled Sophie. "We'll come. I can't wait! My own Sew Zoey dress *and* Cody Calloway! This is the best night ever!"

Libby looked at Zoey over Sophie's head and smiled gratefully. *Thank you!* Libby mouthed. Zoey shook her head, indicating it was no big deal. Sophie was cute and funny, and she seemed to adore Zoey. It would be fun to make her an outfit.

All of a sudden, the lights went out, and a huge roar came from the crowd. Cody Calloway was about to come on!

Zoey and Libby instinctively reached for each other's hands behind Sophie's back and squeezed. They were about to see Cody, *live*, onstage.

The bass line to one of his best songs came on, and Zoey heard herself, and most of the crowd, start to sing along.

Two hours later, the concert was over. Zoey had sung herself hoarse, and Sophie was so tired, she was resting her head against Zoey's shoulder. The crowd from the stadium was slowly moving toward the exits, and after helping Sophie up, Mrs. Flynn began guiding the girls to the exit nearest their seats.

In the lobby of the arena, people had set up booths selling T-shirts and other Cody Calloway memorabilia. Libby and Sophie paused to look at a few things when Zoey saw a booth with a huge sign that read, THE CAMP OF ROCK! Curious, Zoey moved closer and picked up a flyer. The Camp of Rock was a weeklong, intensive camp for middle school and high school students with rock bands. It culminated in an outdoor concert for the young musician campers that featured a mystery big-name headliner band dropping in to play a few songs. And camp started in just over a week!

On impulse, Zoey folded the flyer and then put it in her pocket. She knew just the person for it.

After Mrs. Flynn dropped Zoey at home, Zoey ran into the house to look for her brother. Marcus's car was in the driveway, which meant he had to be home from his date with Allie. She found him in the basement, strumming his new guitar and watching a movie on TV. He usually played the drums but had recently picked up the guitar, too.

Zoey unfolded the flyer and then handed it to him. "Look," she said. "You should do this!"

"'*The Camp of Rock*'?" he read. Silently, he

scanned the rest of the flyer. Then he looked up at Zoey questioningly.

"Your band has been practicing so much this summer!" she said. "The Space Invaders are really sounding good."

Marcus chewed his lip and read over the flyer again. "I don't know," he said. "We've only been playing together for a while. It takes a long time to get ready for something like this. What if they reject us?"

Zoey shrugged. "So they reject you. So what? You'll never know if you don't send in an application!"

"Easy for you to say," Marcus grumbled.

"Listen, Kate told me yesterday that the reason she's a great athlete is because she doesn't waste time overthinking. So I'm telling you to do the same. Just apply, Marcus! See what happens!"

Zoey watched her brother's face as he thought it over. Zoey really believed her brother was a talented musician, but she also knew he wasn't someone with a big ego who automatically thought he was the best at everything. Zoey understood that; she was the same way. She'd been lucky with her design business; she had some great mentors, like Fashionsista, Jan from A Stitch in Time, and Allie, who encouraged her to aim high.

Marcus sighed. "The application is due *tomorrow*, Zo. How can I get it done in time?"

Zoey smiled confidently. "You will. Don't think, just *do*."

Marcus rolled his eyes at her. "All right—I'll *think* about it, okay? And I'll call the band tomorrow to talk it over."

"Cool," Zoey said. She yawned. "I'm off to bed. Cody was so great, and I'm exhausted!"

"Wash my shirt!" Marcus called as she headed upstairs. "I want it clean and back in my room by tomorrow!"

"No problem," Zoey yelled back. "It'll be ready for you to wear to rock camp next week!"

-------- CHAPTER 3 --------

Cheers for Cherries!

Do you like this sketch? I'm going peach picking today with my friend Priti. I've had this fabric with cherries on it forever and didn't know what to do with it, so I'm making myself a pair of high-waisted shorts. (And, yes, I know cherries and peaches are not the same fruit, but fashion doesn't have to be totally literal, right??!) ☺ The shorts are turning out so cute, I might wear them with tights this fall!

And speaking of things I might do, I'm pretty sure I'm FINALLY ready to mail my letter to Fashionsista. My brother and his band might apply to a rock camp, and I know how much courage that takes, so I feel like I need to show a little courage as well! After all, what's the worst that could happen?

(Don't answer that!!!!!)

After breakfast, Zoey parked herself at the dining room table with her sewing machine and fabric, ready to finish the cherry-patterned shorts. Priti and her mom would be picking her up in an hour or two to head to the farm, and Zoey wanted her shorts to be done and ironed by then.

Marcus had been sitting in the living room all morning, filling out the application for the Camp of Rock, which he'd downloaded from their website. He was muttering under his breath as he did it—something about how people should never listen to their little sisters.

"Don't worry, Marcus," Zoey called from the dining room. "You'll get it done."

Marcus walked over to Zoey. "It has to be postmarked *today*," he reminded her. "And it's long! Both of my bandmates have weekend jobs and I asked Allie to come over and help, but she said she had a bunch of stuff to finish and mail off for her accessories site. So now I'm doing it all myself."

"Do you want me to help?" Zoey asked.

"Nah," Marcus said sheepishly. "I guess I just felt like venting. It's getting there."

Zoey grinned broadly. "Okay, well, if you change your mind, I'm right here."

She returned to her sewing, humming quietly to herself. Sewing had become such a big part of her life that she was used to waking up on Saturday and Sunday mornings with piles of "work" to do. But to Zoey it wasn't work. It was her passion! If she could sew all day, every day, she would. And she knew Marcus felt the same way about his band. He just needed some encouragement.

A little while later, Zoey happened to look out the front window and see the postman across the street, a few houses up. He would be at their door any minute to deliver the mail.

"Marcus! The mailman is at the McCuddy's house!" She pointed, and Marcus looked up, alarmed.

"Okay, I guess I can send it," he said. "I was just reading it over." He hurriedly folded the application and shoved it into an envelope he'd already prepared with the address and a stamp. "Wow—I guess I'm really doing it!" he said with a triumphant look at Zoey.

It gave Zoey the final push she needed. She would be brave, just as she was telling her brother to be. She dashed up to her room, retrieved the letter she'd written to Daphne Shaw, and flew back downstairs.

"Here," she said breathlessly, handing the small envelope to Marcus. "Mail this too, okay? It's important."

Marcus nodded, flinging open the door and running to meet the postman.

Zoey shut the door behind him and ran up to her room to send a text to her friends to tell them she'd finally done it—she'd mailed the letter! Just as she was pressing send, she heard a knock on the door.

She ran back downstairs to find her brother, who'd gotten a call from Allie while he was talking to the postman, and somehow had locked himself out of the house.

He shrugged sheepishly at his sister as she let him in, and gave her a high five.

"I did it," he said.

"We both did," she replied. "Phew!"

"Remind me again why we're picking peaches?" Zoey asked a few hours later as she and Priti sat in a large field, enjoying the sun and fresh air. There were about a dozen other people there as well, including Priti's mother, who was wearing a straw hat and gardening gloves and who looked as if she were in heaven.

Priti started to laugh but then stopped herself. "My mom has been trying to come up with 'special' things we can do together, now that my dad's moved out. Like, when I'm at our house on 'her' time, we can't just be normal—we have to spend quality time together."

Zoey looked around thoughtfully. The orchard was beautiful, and it was a perfect late summer day to be outside. "It could be worse," Zoey said. "Quality time could have been grocery shopping or something."

Priti giggled. "Yeah, or how about mopping the floors?"

"Or polishing the silver."

"Or cleaning the gutters!"

The girls laughed hardest at that one and then went back to picking peaches for several minutes. When Zoey had filled a few baskets, she sat back and pulled out her sketchbook from her knapsack.

"Working on something new?" Priti asked.

Zoey shrugged. "Just some ideas for back-to-school outfits. I made these shorts this morning—do you like them?"

Priti nodded enthusiastically. "LOVE them. The cherries are so cute! And the high waist is really fun, too."

From two rows over, Mrs. Holbrooke called, "Girls, are you having fun? Shall we stay a bit longer?"

Priti and Zoey looked at each other and nodded, since it was obvious from the giant smile on Mrs. Holbrooke's face that she was enjoying herself. And Zoey had to admit, she was having a much better time than she'd anticipated. Being outside and chatting with a good friend was definitely a nice way to spend the day.

"If you're supposed to be having quality time with your mom, why am I here?" Zoey whispered.

Priti looked guilty. "I begged her to let you come too. I don't like quality time! It feels so forced. She's my *mom*. We live together. And now we have to go and pick fruit? Can't we just talk to each other? My sisters are in high school, so they don't have to do all this stuff—they're too 'old.' It's just me."

It was hard for Zoey to hear Priti like this. Priti was always her happiest, most cheerful, most glass-is-half-full friend. Zoey put down her sketchbook and sat next to Priti.

"I'm here if you need me," she said, wishing she had something more to offer.

Priti half smiled. "I know you are. Thanks." She fiddled with her friendship bracelet—the one made with beads to represent her, Zoey, Kate, and Libby, the one that each girl had—turning it around and around her wrist. "Oh, so listen to this! Remember I told you my dad's all moved into his new apartment, right? And we're supposed to split time between his place and my mom's until they have a formal custody agreement? He told me he really wants me to decorate my room there *so it feels like home!*"

Priti said the last part in disbelief, as if she couldn't imagine ever feeling that a room in an apartment somewhere could be her home. Zoey knew Priti's house, the one where her family had lived since she was a toddler, would always be the place Priti called home.

"But, wait, Priti—think about the positive! It would be so much fun to decorate a room from scratch! It's a totally empty room, so you can dream up anything you want and make it happen. Imagine the room of your dreams!"

Zoey's eyes glowed at the thought. She loved

her own room, but a lot of it was hand-me-down furniture from her grandparents, and curtains that her mother had made when Zoey was a baby. She wouldn't ever get rid of them, because they'd been made for her by her mother, even though the fabric was starting to feel a little babyish.

Priti thought it over, and suddenly her face broke into a huge grin. "You're right, Zo! I could make the room of my dreams. But only," she said, pausing for emphasis, "if *you* help me!"

"Me?" said Zoey. "But I'm a *clothes* designer. Not an interior decorator."

"Doesn't matter," said Priti. "You have great ideas. And I'll need help! I need your vision. Okay? Promise you will! Promise? I want it to be bright and sparkly and fun!"

Zoey couldn't help laughing. "Of course you do, Priti. That sounds just like you." She took a second to think over the idea and then nodded. "Okay, I'll do it. But I'm going to ask Aunt Lulu to help too, because she knows so much more about this, and I really want you to love it. Deal?"

"Deal!" Priti squealed with joy, the happiest

Zoey had heard her since they'd returned from camp. Priti was so delighted, in fact, that she flung herself on Zoey, attempting to give her a huge hug but accidentally knocking her to the ground.

Zoey groaned. "*Owwww*. I think we landed on my peaches."

Priti giggled. "I guess we need to pick more, then!"

"We do," Zoey agreed. "At least my shorts are patterned. Maybe the stains will blend in!"

Zoey didn't know what to do with all the peaches she'd picked at the farm, and decided a brunch party might be fun. She asked her dad if he liked the idea, and he did, so later that afternoon Zoey called her aunt Lulu and invited her to Sunday brunch the next day. Lulu accepted the invitation, with the caveat that she would be bringing someone special with her—her new boyfriend.

Zoey agreed immediately, even though she wasn't quite sure how she felt about sharing her favorite aunt. She knew Aunt Lulu had been married once before, but Zoey had only been about two or three when Lulu had gotten divorced, and since then, Lulu spent most of her time and energy building her interior design business. Her house was always open to Zoey for snacks, impromptu visits, and sleepovers, not to mention Camp Lulu! Zoey noticed that since she'd returned from sleepaway camp, Lulu seemed busier and more preoccupied than usual, and Zoey wondered if her boyfriend was the reason.

On Sunday morning Zoey took a shower and then hurried downstairs. She wanted to set the table extra nicely for their guests, and she planned to make delicious peach pancakes for breakfast. She was even going to freshly squeeze orange juice.

Her father was already in the kitchen, drinking coffee and reading the paper, when she burst into the kitchen, ready to begin.

"Morning, sweetie," he said. "You're up early."

"Aunt Lulu and her boyfriend are coming over, remember?"

Her father nodded. "Of course I remember. I

made an extra large pot of coffee, and I even picked some hydrangeas from the garden to put on the table. They're Lulu's favorite. I stuck them in that vase, but I'm sure you can do a better job of arranging them than I can."

Zoey couldn't help smiling. Lulu was her mother's sister, but since Zoey's mother had died when Zoey was young, Lulu had become a big part of their little family. Zoey knew that her dad loved Lulu more like a real sister than a sister-in-law.

Normally, Zoey and Marcus took turns making Sunday pancakes with their dad, and today would have been Marcus's turn. But Zoey could hear Marcus playing drums in the basement, and she wasn't sure he'd want to be disturbed. He had four more days to wait until he'd hear about his rock camp application, and Zoey knew he was very nervous. So she started to get out the ingredients for the pancake batter and decided she'd let him do next weekend's turn.

"How about I make the pancakes, and you set the table?" her dad suggested. "You always do a great job of making things beautiful, Zo. And we want to impress Lulu's friend."

"We do?" Zoey asked. She wasn't used to Aunt Lulu having a boyfriend, and a part of her worried that her special connection with her aunt might change.

Her father nodded firmly. "Yes. Lately, Lulu has been the happiest I've seen her in ages. So let's be as welcoming as possible, all right?"

"Of course, Dad. Good idea!"

Zoey quickly went to clear the dining room table of her sewing things. The family normally ate in the kitchen and let the dining room be considered as "Zoey's office," but for Lulu, Zoey wanted to host the perfect brunch. If her dad wanted them to be welcoming, then that's what they would be.

His name was John Chadden, and he sold software. Lulu and John knocked on the front door instead of just walking in, as Zoey's aunt normally would do. When Zoey answered the door, John held it open for Lulu and ushered her in, like a princess. Lulu's cheeks were pink, and she wore a dress Zoey had never seen before.

John shook hands with Mr. Webber and Marcus, whom he'd met already, and then turned to Zoey.

John smiled, looking somewhat nervous, and said, "It's great to finally meet you, Zoey. You're practically famous! Lulu talks of nothing but you and Marcus. I know all about your blog and your Etsy site and your beautiful designs. Really, we might as well just eat, because there's nothing you can possibly tell me about yourself that Lulu hasn't already."

Zoey couldn't help feeling flattered. Lulu blushed again at John's teasing, and Marcus and Mr. Webber burst out laughing. Lulu was a talker, that's for sure, but Zoey felt certain she wasn't the only one in her family who was pleased Lulu discussed them all in such detail. They were as special to her as she was to them. Maybe this John wouldn't change that at all.

Zoey sat next to Lulu during brunch and was delighted by how well the peach pancakes went over. As Marcus was filling in his father and John on some of the details about his rock camp application, Zoey leaned toward her aunt.

"Aunt Lulu?" she said. "I have a few small favors to ask you."

Lulu smiled and then dabbed at her mouth with her napkin. "You can ask me a few big favors, if you want to."

Zoey grinned. "Well, first, I'm making a dress for my friend Libby's sister, Sophie, and Mrs. Flynn wants to come over on Monday to talk about it. And second, my friend Priti—you know Priti— Her parents have just split up, and her dad has a new apartment now. And he said she can decorate her new room any way she wants. But she doesn't know where to begin! So I said I'd help her, but I think I'm going to need a lot of advice from you to do it right. I want this room to be perfect for her, so she feels at home when she's staying with her dad."

Lulu agreed immediately. "Of course the Flynns can come over and of course I'll help! I adore Priti. Such a cheerful spirit. We'll have to use lots of bright colors for that girl. How about you start getting some ideas from her, and then we'll make a plan when you come over this week. Sound good?"

Zoey nodded and leaned toward her aunt again, except this time for a hug. It wasn't just a thank-you hug, either, and Lulu seemed to sense that.

"You'll always be my girl, Zoey," Aunt Lulu whispered. "No matter who else comes along."

It was a lovely brunch indeed.

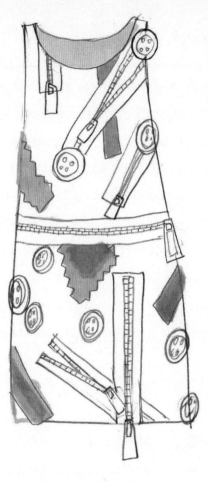

----------- CHAPTER 4 -----------

Summer Lovin', Happened So Fast . . .

I can't believe it! My aunt Lulu is in luuuv. I can tell even by the clothes she's been wearing—bright and cheerful and feminine! She's still Aunt Lulu, though, and she's agreed (thankfully!) to help me with my brand-new project—decorating my friend Priti's new bedroom! To celebrate my new side career as an interior decorator, I'm making this awesome decorator's dress, complete with fabric samples attached to it, and lots of baubles and zippers. It's like a concept board, right on the dress! Yes, it's more whimsical than practical, but then shouldn't all great design have a note of whimsy? I think *sew!*

On a side note—mission accomplished—I finally mailed that letter to the person I think is Fashionsista. Full disclosure: My brother mailed it for me. Now the waiting begins for a reply . . . but at least I can say it's in the mail!

On Monday Zoey went to Aunt Lulu's, as she normally did in the summers when her dad was at work. Lulu popped in and out during the day, depending on how busy her schedule was, but her dog, Buttons, was there, and Zoey enjoyed taking him for walks and having his company while she sewed. She also loved to flip through Lulu's stash of clothing and design magazines. She planned to ask Lulu if she could take a few home to study for ideas for Priti's room.

Zoey spent most of the morning working on

her decorator's dress, which she knew might not be something she'd wear a lot but loved the idea so much, she just wanted to try it. She was working in Lulu's dining room, with fabric samples and buttons everywhere, when Mrs. Flynn, Sophie, and Libby arrived to discuss Sophie's back-to-school dress.

Zoey flew to the door to greet them. She loved meeting with customers and having the chance to feel like a real designer. Libby gave Zoey a big hug, as if thanking her in advance for what Zoey was doing for Sophie.

Zoey ushered everyone into Lulu's beautiful living room and then asked them to sit down.

"Where do we begin?" asked Mrs. Flynn. She and Libby looked expectantly at Zoey, as if waiting for detailed instructions.

Zoey smiled and turned to Sophie. "How about you tell me what you like," Zoey said to her, sitting down with her sketchbook and pencil. "I've already thought a bit about what might work, but I want to make sure it's what you want."

Sophie, who hadn't said a word since they'd arrived because she'd been so busy looking around at all the beautiful things in Lulu's house, appeared delighted to suddenly have all the attention on her.

"I'm not sure," she began shyly. "But I like lots of colors. And patterns. And I want it to be comfortable, so I can do monkey bars on the playground, but also really cute, because all the girls wear cute dresses to school on the first day."

Zoey nodded and started moving her pencil across the paper. "Do you like ruffles? Buttons? Pockets?"

Sophie nodded. "Yes, I like all those things!"

"She does," Libby confirmed. "Sophie reeeeally loves ruffles."

Zoey continued sketching for several minutes and then moved position so Libby, Sophie, and Mrs. Flynn could all see her sketch pad.

"I'm thinking something like this," she began, "so it's loose enough for her to put a long-sleeve tee under it later this fall if she wants to, which will make it more casual. And then the top of the dress is one fabric, with a seam across *here* to the main fabric. At the bottom, there would be a third fabric, so it'd be three panels. Like color blocking, but with different patterned fabrics. It'll be really cheery and fun and won't look like anyone else's dress!"

"But what color will it be?" Sophie asked. "My favorites are white, purple, red, silver, and blue."

Zoey laughed. "It can be *all* of those, or just some. You can help me pick the fabrics! I'll go to the fabric store and find a bunch of great swatches for you to choose from, and then I'll start making the dress, okay?"

Sophie nodded, looking pleased. Zoey noticed Libby smiling, too, like she was happy to see her little sister behaving so well.

Zoey retrieved her tape measure from the dining room and started to measure Sophie, jotting the numbers down on the sketch pad.

"Shall I give you some money now for the swatches?" asked Mrs. Flynn.

"What's a *swatch*?" Sophie asked suddenly.

"A swatch," said Zoey, "is a little sample of fabric that people use to pick and choose what will work for them without having to buy a whole yard. And fabric swatches are free! So don't worry."

"Oh, that's nice," said Mrs. Flynn. "I was shopping

for carpet for my bedroom last year, and I had to pay ten dollars for a carpet sample I could bring home and test with my paint colors. It's a good thing I did, though, because the carpet looked hideous with my walls! So I guess samples are a good thing."

"And with fabric they're free!" said Zoey. "Which is even better."

"I do want to pay you for your work, though," Mrs. Flynn added hastily. "Whatever you charge customers on your Etsy site is fine."

Zoey shook her head. "No, thank you. It's a pleasure to make an outfit for my friend Sophie! And you did take me to the amazing Cody Calloway concert the other night."

Mrs. Flynn nodded slightly. "Well, all right. But if you end up making another outfit for Sophie in the future, I insist on paying. It's important to support young artists."

"Young *artists*!" Sophie giggled. "That sounds like Zoey is painting or something."

"There are many forms of art," Mrs. Flynn explained, "and clothing design is certainly one of them!"

Zoey nodded and smiled. She was thrilled to be referred to as a young artist. After all, that's what she was. And she was proud of her work and how much she'd been able to accomplish so far.

Zoey picked up her sketch pad again to jot down a few more notes, and Mrs. Flynn stood up and strolled around Aunt Lulu's living room.

"This house is really beautiful," Mrs. Flynn said. "You know, I gave up on my bedroom redo after that carpet sample didn't work out, and I just love your aunt's taste. Do you think . . ."

Just then the front door opened and Aunt Lulu walked in, home from a client meeting. She looked surprised for a second to see so many people in her living room, as if maybe she'd walked into the wrong house by mistake. Then she slapped her forehead, suddenly remembering that Zoey had asked her if she could have the Flynns over.

"Hello, everyone!" Lulu said. "Sorry to look so shocked. I was in a fog thinking about a client. You must be the Flynns."

Zoey quickly introduced her aunt to everyone. "Aunt Lulu, this is my friend Libby and her mother,

Mrs. Flynn. I'm making Libby's little sister a back-to-school dress, and we were just discussing our plan."

"It's a real pleasure to meet you, Lulu," said Mrs. Flynn. "I can't stop admiring your house!"

"Thank you." Aunt Lulu smiled broadly and shook Mrs. Flynn's hand. "Compliments are one thing I can never get enough of. Make yourselves at home! Look around."

"What's this?" asked a small voice coming from Lulu's office.

With Aunt Lulu's sudden arrival, Zoey had completely forgotten about Sophie, who'd darted off to Lulu's office, unnoticed.

The group all headed into the office to find Sophie enthralled with a large inspiration board Lulu had created for a client.

"That's a concept board, or inspiration board," Lulu explained. "I cover it with pictures of furniture, art, lamps, and samples of fabric, as well as wallpaper scraps and paint colors. It makes it easier to imagine how a room will look when it's done if I can make it out of tiny scraps and pictures first!"

"I love all the little pictures and fabrics. It's

so beautiful!" Sophie said breathlessly.

Sophie kept touching one piece in particular, a sample of a herringbone material representing the rug that Lulu intended to use for the client.

Seeing this, Lulu went to one of her books of swatches and located the herringbone fabric. She cut out a neat square and presented it to Sophie.

"This is for you," Lulu said, "to start your own inspiration board at home. All right?"

Sophie was so thrilled, she could hardly speak. She held the swatch in her hand like it was a giant cone of cotton candy. Her eyes glowing, she whispered "thank you" to Aunt Lulu.

"That's very kind," said Mrs. Flynn. "You know, I'd really love to talk to you about redecorating some rooms in my house. Do you have a few minutes now?"

Aunt Lulu clapped her hands. "Absolutely! Let's go back to the living room, and I'll make some coffee. Zoey, Libby—why don't you take Buttons outside for some playtime? He's been chewing on the kitchen table's legs lately when he doesn't get enough exercise."

"Can I go outside with the girls?" Sophie asked her mother hopefully.

Mrs. Flynn looked at Libby, who shook her head slightly. Zoey wasn't sure why Libby didn't want Sophie to come, but she assumed Libby needed a break from her, as she'd mentioned before. Zoey sort of enjoyed Sophie's six-year-old enthusiasm and sweetness, but maybe it was hard to take all day, every day.

"Stay inside with us, Sophie," her mother said. "I've got some crayons for you to color with while Lulu and I talk."

"*Okay,*" said Sophie, somewhat offended. "I'd rather color, anyway."

"I'll set you up in the office with scissors and paper, Sophie," Lulu said nicely. "And maybe some cookies, too."

The next day Zoey was at Aunt Lulu's again, sewing an item for her Sew Zoey store on Etsy. She didn't keep a stock of items to sell, so whenever an order came in, it had to be made especially for the customer and then shipped out. She had a few different designs on her site that were available to order, and after doing each one several times, she was getting pretty fast at making them. But it still made her feel frantic sometimes when she saw that a new order had come in and she'd have to make a whole piece and ship it out within a few days!

Lulu happened to be home and was working on a new inspiration board for someone. She sat near Zoey and her sewing. This was one of the things Zoey loved about working at Camp Lulu's. There was a camaraderie in working alongside someone else, especially when both were doing creative work, and there was nothing more fun than when Aunt Lulu suggested they run out to a café for lunch together. Zoey was glad that having a boyfriend hadn't changed Camp Lulu.

"How's John?" Zoey asked.

Aunt Lulu took a breath before answering, and smiled. "Oh, he's just, well, wonderful. I hope you liked him." She looked at Zoey searchingly, as if the answer were very, very important.

Zoey smiled back at her aunt. "*Of course* I liked him. I thought he was great! And he definitely seemed to adore you. Although, why wouldn't he? You're Lulu!"

Aunt Lulu laughed. "Oh, Zoey, I hope *you* have a niece someday. There really is nothing better."

"I hope so, too," Zoey said. "I'd love to have my own Camp Zoey for her! I'll probably still be working on this Etsy order. . . ."

Aunt Lulu leaned over to inspect the blouse that Zoey was carefully basting together. "How's the Etsy site doing these days?"

Zoey frowned, pensive. "Not as well as I'd like. I had to take some time off while I was at camp, and I only have a few pieces on there, ones I'm really good at making, so I don't have very many customers. It's nowhere near as easy as the accessories site."

Lulu nodded thoughtfully. "Well, it's much harder for people to buy clothing online. They have no idea if it will fit, especially if it's not a regular store brand that they're used to. So it makes sense you'd have fewer orders."

"Mostly, I keep getting requests from this one customer—Dakota Brown. This shirt is for her, actually. She seems to be my biggest fan!"

"One fan, especially a devoted one, isn't bad," said Lulu. "It sure beats none!"

She and Zoey laughed together. Zoey knew Lulu was right—it was great to have someone who kept buying clothes from her site. That obviously meant that what she was making was being worn and enjoyed by someone. But Zoey couldn't help wanting more for her Etsy site. Though how she'd do it, she didn't know.

"Let's plan a business lunch soon," Aunt Lulu suggested. "Just you and me. We'll go out and talk about some marketing you could do for your site, or ways you could beef it up. Sound good?"

"Good? That sounds *awesome*!" Zoey said. "Thanks, Aunt Lulu!"

"And in the meantime, remember that you have a *second* devoted fan right here, got it?"

"Got it," said Zoey.

It was a very pleasant day at Camp Lulu.

------------- CHAPTER 5 -----------

Projects Here, Projects There, Projects, Projects EVERYWHERE!

This sketch is for a six-year-old girl who's tall for her age and likely to grow even more this fall! I'm trying to find the right style of dress to work for her, while also being fully functional on the monkey bars (her request!).

I love the color-blocking style of the patterned fabrics—it feels fresh and young and fun for this little lady!

Even though it's summertime, when most people hang out and relax by the pool, I've suddenly found myself working on this dress for a friend, designing a bedroom for another friend (!), and filling two orders from my Etsy site! It makes me think: I've been dying to get some more business for my site, but if I do, when will I find time to make the clothes, what with school starting again soon? I guess that would be what my dad calls "a good problem to have." Readers, if you have ideas for how I can improve my Sew Zoey store, please comment and let me know! I'd love your advice!

Zoey and Aunt Lulu decided to visit their favorite fabric store, A Stitch in Time, the next day. Zoey needed swatches to show Sophie for her dress, as well as a bunch of fabrics and buttons and accessories for the concept she and Aunt Lulu had discussed for Priti's bedroom. Luckily, the store's manager, Jan, was there and was able to help them select a ton of great options. Zoey left with a giant bag filled with beautiful samples and swatches to show her friends.

Aunt Lulu offered to drive Zoey to Mrs. Flynn's house right after their shopping trip, so Zoey could get approval on fabrics for Sophie's dress. Aunt Lulu also wanted to take a look at the rooms Mrs. Flynn was considering redecorating.

While Aunt Lulu toured the house, taking notes, Zoey plopped down on the sofa with her bag of goodies and began showing fabric samples to Mrs. Flynn and Sophie.

Mrs. Flynn was impressed. "They're all so beautiful, Zoey! I just know this dress will be amazing."

"A Stitch in Time has the best fabrics," Zoey told her.

Sophie pulled out about seven of the swatches and spread them in front of her. She kept touching each one in a row, over and over again.

"I can't decide," she said, looking to Zoey for help. "I like them all!"

Zoey grinned at her. "I like them all too. But don't worry—even if we don't use some for this dress, they'll still have the fabric at the store. We could always make you something else later with one of the swatches we don't choose. Okay?"

Sophie nodded, her eyes huge from all the options before her.

Zoey picked three of the fabrics and held them up together. "I was thinking maybe these three," she suggested. "With this one on top, this one in the middle, and this one on the bottom. Wouldn't they look nice together?"

Sophie nodded, and Mrs. Flynn quickly agreed. "We're lucky to have you, Zoey," she said.

"*Very* lucky," Libby echoed.

Zoey blushed slightly. It was nice to have clients so appreciative of her work, and she hadn't even made the dress yet! She'd really have to make it one of her best ever.

"I'm going to buy the fabrics and start sewing, and then let's have another fitting next week to make sure it's perfect, all right?" Zoey asked.

"I agree," said Mrs. Flynn. "I just measured Miss Sophie against the kitchen wall last night, and she's already a teeny bit taller than she was at her last checkup!"

Sophie shrugged, still enthralled by all the fabrics in Zoey's bag.

Mrs. Flynn looked at her fondly. "You know, Zoey, since we came to your aunt's house, all Sophie has talked about is becoming an interior or fashion designer. I think you've really sparked something in her!"

Zoey turned to Sophie, who was looking down shyly, much like her older sister, Libby, often did. "That's great, Sophie!" Zoey said encouragingly. "You're never too young to start."

"That's what I keep telling her," said Mrs. Flynn.

Suddenly, Zoey noticed something odd about Mrs. Flynn.

"Um, Mrs. Flynn?" she said tentatively. "One of your earrings is missing!"

Mrs. Flynn's hand shot up to feel each of her ears. Then she started laughing when she realized she was only wearing one gold, dangly chandelier earring.

"I was looking for the match this morning and couldn't find it. And then I had to rush Libby off to ballet camp! I meant to change my earrings when I got home, but I got busy doing other things. How does it look with just the one? Stylish?"

Zoey laughed and nodded her head. "I think you're going to start a new trend."

"Speaking of trends," Libby said. "Since you're already here, Zoey, would you come up to my room for a minute and look at the new skirt my mom just bought me for school? I need your opinion on what to wear with it."

Zoey grinned. "Of course! I'd love to see it."

"Can I come too?" Sophie asked hopefully.

Libby frowned slightly, and Mrs. Flynn noticed, because she said, very gently, "Sophie, stay down here with me and let the big girls have a minute, okay?"

Sophie nodded, and watched mournfully as Zoey and Libby headed upstairs. Zoey heard the phone ring, and Mrs. Flynn headed to the kitchen to answer it.

It's not easy being a little sister, Zoey thought.

On Thursday evening Zoey was at home in the dining room–sewing office when there was a knock at the door. She was about to get up and answer it when she heard Marcus's feet thundering up the basement steps and racing to the foyer. She heard him open the door and listened hard to hear who was there.

She heard a few mumbled hellos, and then Allie's voice saying, "Congratulations! I'm so happy the Space Invaders made it!"

Made it? *The Space Invaders?*

Zoey hopped up and ran to the front door herself, not caring at all that she was interrupting her brother as he was hugging his girlfriend.

"Marcus," she said breathlessly. "Your band made the cut? You're doing the Camp of Rock?"

Marcus's cheeks were red, and he looked happy, but he shook his head. "Not quite," he explained. "We made the first cut, which was the paper application, and now we have to do a live audition."

"But you're halfway there!" Zoey couldn't help squealing a little, just as she had at the Cody Calloway concert. Good news was good news, even if he still had one more hurdle to jump. "How come you didn't tell me right away?"

Marcus put up his hands and looked at the ceiling. "I don't know—I had to call the band and Dad and Allie, and I just forgot. I'm sorry. You know how distracted I've been."

Zoey frowned. Yes, she did know, but she'd been sitting right upstairs in the dining room and he hadn't told her. Could her brother really be *that* spacey?

And then Zoey remembered something— her letter to Daphne Shaw. Marcus had mailed it nearly a week ago and she hadn't heard anything in response. Had Marcus *actually* mailed it? How could she know for sure? He'd obviously mailed his band application, but he'd also taken a call from Allie when he was talking to the mailman and had gotten locked out of the house. What if he'd dropped the letter or put it in his pocket by mistake?

You're letting your imagination get carried away, Zoey told herself, before she almost opened her mouth to accuse her brother right in front of Allie. *It's very possible he mailed it and Daphne just hasn't had a chance to respond yet. Or maybe she's writing back a nice, long, snail-mail letter, instead of an e-mail. It could be anything.*

While Zoey was mulling over her letter, Marcus said, "I've got to go practice. I've got a live audition next week! Allie, come downstairs and listen."

Allie smiled at him sweetly. "I will, but first let me catch up with Zoey for a few minutes, and then I'll be right down. Okay?"

Marcus agreed reluctantly and left the girls alone. Zoey was pleased Allie wanted to hang out with just her for a few minutes. After all, Allie had been *her* friend first—not to mention her former business partner.

Zoey gestured to the sofa and said, "Sit! I've got an awesome bag of samples to show you for some projects I'm working on. I'm even designing a bedroom for a friend of mine!"

Allie sat down, and Zoey went to the dining room to retrieve her bag of swatches. She dumped everything out on the coffee table in front of Allie. She outlined the design concept for Priti's room and showed Allie the fabrics she was thinking of using. It was nice to have another designer to discuss her ideas with.

Allie gushed over everything. "Look at these

buttons! You're going to use these on some bed pillows?"

The buttons were round and silver and reflective, like little mirrors. They were *very* Priti. "Yes," said Zoey. "Those will go on two big pillows on the bed, and I'm going to trim the pillows with *this* ribbon."

"I love that, too!" Allie said. "Wow. Those go together so well. I have *just* the project for these buttons—they're fabulous." She held two of the buttons in her hands, watching as they reflected back the light.

Zoey was pleased her choices were such a hit. She still hadn't shown them to Priti yet, so it was great to get all this positive feedback from someone with such good taste!

"I got them all at A Stitch in Time," Zoey said. "Although they didn't have many of those mirror buttons left, so if you want some, you should go soon."

Allie nodded. "I will."

Zoey started to pack all her stuff back into the bag, and Allie helped.

When they were almost finished, Allie turned to Zoey and said, "I want to ask you something."

"Um, okay." Zoey sat back down, nervous, unsure why Allie sounded so serious. Was something wrong?

Allie took a deep breath. "I want to make something really special for Marcus's band's audition, but I don't know what. Some kind of accessory. Do you have any ideas?"

Zoey immediately felt guilty that she hadn't thought to do that first. After all, Marcus was her brother! But then again, she'd only found out about the audition a few minutes ago, and Marcus had completely forgotten to even tell her about it.

Zoey shook her head. "No, not really, but I can try to think of some. Although, I'm sure Marcus would love whatever you made him!"

Allie smiled tightly. Sighing, she said, "Well, he's been a little, um, annoyed with me, because I've been so busy lately making items for my Etsy site. I wasn't able to help with his camp application, but you know how it is, Zoey. School's starting soon, and I've got to stock up on some of my hard-to-make stuff, so that I'll be able to keep up after classes begin."

Zoey nodded, understanding, even though she didn't have much demand for her own store yet. "Totally! And I'm sure Marcus knows that. He's so proud of you! He talks about your site all the time and how awesome your designs are."

"Well, I just want to make sure he knows I support him and his band," Allie said. She looked at Zoey and smiled ruefully. "I really like him," she added quietly.

"I know," said Zoey. "He likes you, too. We'll think of something great you can make for him, okay? But right now, you should probably go down and listen to him practice. He loves an audience."

Zoey giggled, and Allie relaxed and laughed also. "Thanks, Zoey," she said. "You're a great sister."

CHAPTER 6

Fun in the Sun!

I've been doing tons of design and planning for the two big projects I'm working on right now, plus the occasional Etsy order, and now I think I'm ready for a day off! Work hard, play hard, right? I'm heading to the beach today with two of my best friends for swimming, sunning, and girl talk. And probably—definitely—some ice cream . . .

I still haven't heard back from the person I *think* is Fashionsista. I'm starting to worry that maybe I have the wrong person . . . or that the letter never arrived. Waiting to hear from her is even harder than deciding whether or not to mail the letter! So, Fashionsista, if you got my letter, please send me a quick e-mail that says, "You've got me!" or something. ☺

Anyhoo, I made myself this cute wrap to wear as a cover-up to the beach today. . . . Do you like it? It's a little different from the usual tunic or T-shirt that most people wear. Hopefully, it'll be a big hit! Maybe I'll even add this as an item to my Etsy store. . . . They're fun to make and easy to size!

Mrs. Mackey pulled up in front of the Webbers' house and beeped her horn. Zoey's dad was at work, and her brother was already at the pool, starting his shift as a lifeguard, so Zoey carefully locked the door and then stumbled down the front walk to the car, weighed down by two large tote bags.

As Zoey climbed into the car, Mrs. Mackey said, "Zoey, what on Earth did you bring with you? I thought I was just taking you girls to the beach for the day!"

Zoey giggled as Kate looked back at her with a grin on her face from the front seat. Zoey knew Kate could guess what Zoey had with her. One bag was her beach bag, with sunscreen, magazines, sunglasses, a hat, a towel, water, and snacks. The other was her work bag, with her sketchbook, her sewing kit "essentials", and all the samples and swatches to show Priti for her new room.

"I like to be prepared," Zoey said. "You never know when you might have a few minutes to get some sewing or sketching done! And of course I have some samples to show Priti."

"Well, I hope you have a first-aid kit in there, too," said Mrs. Mackey. "My poor Kate seems to be on a run of bad luck."

"What do you mean?" asked Zoey, immediately concerned. She scooted forward in her seat and leaned to the right, so she could see Kate better. To her surprise, Kate was wearing a sling on her arm, the same arm she'd hurt last spring during a soccer game.

"Kate!" Zoey exclaimed. "What happened? Why didn't you tell me?"

Kate grimaced. "I haven't told anyone yet. Nothing happened—specifically. I've got swimmer's shoulder from overtraining. Normally, you can just rest it and ice it, but my coach wants me to be extra careful and keep it in a sling for a while, and take a temporary break from swimming. She thinks it'll heal better that way."

"Oh, Kate, I'm so sorry," Zoey said.

"It's all right," Kate replied. "Really. I'll be fine soon."

Kate was trying her best to sound cheerful, but Zoey knew how much Kate loved swimming. Having just been voted team captain must have made her enforced rest particularly hard to bear.

They picked up Priti and then headed for the beach—Libby was in ballet camp all day and couldn't make it.

Kate relayed the same story about her shoulder to Priti, who was equally sympathetic. Priti and

Zoey exchanged a look in the backseat that said they knew Kate had more to say about her injury, but she probably didn't want to say it in front of her mother, who tended to worry.

When they arrived at the beach, Mrs. Mackey parked and then told the girls she planned to do some shopping and have a nice lunch somewhere. "I'll let you girls lie on the beach and catch up. But call or text if you need me or want me to bring you anything, okay? Does everyone have water? And money for food from the Snack Shack?"

The girls all nodded, and then, weighed down by their bags and towels, walked out to the beach. It was a beautiful summer day, warm and breezy, which kept the sun from feeling too hot. Since it was a weekday, the beach wasn't too crowded. They were able to find a spot to spread out with no one else nearby.

Once they were comfortably settled on their towels and covered in sunscreen, Zoey said, "We're sorry about your shoulder, Kate. Do you want to talk about it? Does it hurt?"

Kate shook her head. "It's not too bad. Well,

sometimes it hurts. But not if I just lay still on my back like this. I can't sleep on my side or my stomach for a while."

"Are you bummed?" Priti asked. "It's so unfair that you're injured again so soon!"

"Well, I'm *more* upset I might not get to be team captain now. I know my shoulder will get better if I let it rest for a while. But will the team still want me as captain? When I can't even swim or compete this fall?"

"What?" asked Zoey. "The whole fall? That's not what you said in the car!"

"Coach isn't sure yet," Kate replied. "I *might* be ready in six weeks, she says, but that sounds like forever to me. I'll miss the first few meets, for sure. What will I do if I can't swim all season?" She sighed mournfully, showing the girls for the first time how truly upset she was about the injury.

"You'll rest and be ready to swim again in just a few weeks, Kate—I know you will!" Zoey said. "And in the meantime I'm going to make you some more sling covers. We can't have you start school wearing that frumpy thing. . . ."

Kate smiled at Zoey's attempted joke and then said, "Thanks, I'd love that. If I can't swim, I guess I can at least be fashionable. Or, you know, fashionable for *me*."

The girls laughed.

"Speaking of fashionable, I almost forgot!" said Zoey. "I've got some awesome stuff to show you guys. . . ."

She grabbed her work tote and opened it. She began pulling out swatches and buttons and ribbons, laying them out on her towel to show the girls how she envisioned Priti's room coming together.

"Oh gosh, I LOVE them!" Priti shouted. "Look at these! And those!" She picked up several ribbons, a few swatches, and one of the mirrored buttons, and suddenly, a gust of wind sent them all flying down the beach. Zoey sprang up to retrieve everything and ended up zigzagging all over the place, trying to pick them up.

When she returned, Kate and Priti were both laughing hysterically while anchoring down the remaining items with sunscreen bottles, magazines, and flip-flops.

"That was so funny, Zoey!" Priti said, still cracking up. "Watching you run after those tiny swatches and ribbons flying everywhere!"

"I've never seen you move so fast!" Kate joked. "You'd beat any track team's best sprinter!"

"Glad I'm entertaining everyone!" Zoey said with a grin. She plopped back down and tried to reorganize her things so she could show Priti her ideas for the room. To her right were the fancy mirrored buttons, but there were only two of them. She was certain she'd bought three at the store. Could the other one still be somewhere on the beach? Zoey got up and did a quick scan, but she didn't see the third shiny, mirrored button. She returned to her towel and sat down. Maybe she'd left one back at home on her worktable, or maybe it had fallen on the floor. She was sure it was somewhere.

She gave Priti a quick overview of the room's scheme, and Priti appeared delighted.

"I love every fabric and every accessory!" Priti said. "The only thing I would say is, don't be shy with the bling! 'Cause you know how I love it."

Zoey smiled. She knew Priti's taste like the back

of her hand. She would make the room as beautiful and blingy as Priti could dream it.

"So you're excited about your new room at your dad's now?" Kate asked. "I know you were kind of, um, uncertain about it before."

Priti groaned slightly and rolled over onto her stomach. She was wearing a really cute tankini in a bright neon green that looked gorgeous against her brown skin and dark hair.

"I feel better about it," said Priti. "I guess. But it's hard getting used to shuttling back and forth between my mom's and dad's places. I have to pack a *huge* bag each time, because I need certain stuff. And when I'm with one parent, I miss the other one! But I feel like I'm not supposed to say that."

"Ugh, I'm sorry, Priti," Kate said sympathetically.

"Me too," said Zoey. "You know you can always stay with me! I'll take permanent custody of you."

Priti laughed in spite of herself. "Thanks, Zoey. I'll think about it." She took a long swig from her water bottle. "There is one thing that's gotten easier, though—both houses are so calm now! There's no more tension or fighting. I don't miss *that* at all, that's for sure."

"It's going to get even easier," Kate said. "You'll all get used to the new routine, and it'll start to feel more normal. Especially when Zoey finishes your gorgeous room!"

"The pressure's on, Zoey," Priti joked. "I hope you can deliver."

Zoey grinned and wiggled her eyebrows up and down. "You know me, Priti, I'm always up for a challenge. Now, I'm burning up out here. Let's go jump in the ocean!"

"I can't swim with my sling!" Kate reminded them.

Zoey shrugged good-naturedly. "So let's wade in the ocean. That's more fun than swimming, anyway. And I don't want to get my hair wet—I spent a lot of time on it this morning."

Zoey pointed to her hair, which was wound into a messy bun at the top of her head. Kate and Priti both laughed, and the three girls walked down to the water's edge together, hand in hand.

Zoey woke the next morning with something weighing heavily on her mind. It was Saturday, which meant it had been a full week since she'd mailed her letter to Daphne Shaw. Zoey knew mail sent from her town to New York City usually only took two days—three days, max—so why hadn't she heard from Daphne? There was so much evidence that proved Daphne was Fashionsista that all fingers really did point to the letter having not gotten mailed.

With a worried mind and a heavy heart, Zoey trudged downstairs and found Marcus eating cereal in the kitchen. Even though she knew she probably shouldn't say anything, she couldn't help herself.

"Uhhh, Marcus?" she said tentatively.

With his mouth full and his eyes on a sheet of music, Marcus mumbled, "Whaaa?"

"Did you *definitely* mail that letter I gave you last weekend, when you were running to meet the postman? Because I haven't gotten a response yet, and it's very strange that I haven't."

Marcus looked up at her, his eyes slightly

unfocused, as if she were pulling him out of a trance. He chewed hard for a second, then swallowed. "Uh, yeah. I did."

"You did? You mailed it? You're *sure*?"

He nodded. "Yep."

Zoey bit her lip. She wanted to believe her brother, she really did. He was normally a pretty reliable brother. But he *had* been distracted that day, and worried about finishing his application, and Allie had called him. What if it fell on the ground somewhere and then just blew into a storm drain? Or someone threw it out?

Zoey couldn't quite let it go. "It's just that I haven't heard back. So I thought maybe it didn't get mailed."

Marcus's eyes finally focused, and he looked hurt. "Why do you think I wouldn't mail your letter? You told me it was important."

Zoey nodded. "I know, I know. It's just that you've been a little weird lately. And totally preoccupied with Allie . . ."

As soon as Zoey said Allie's name, she remembered something else—Allie playing with one of the mirrored buttons when she was at Zoey's house a few days ago. Zoey hadn't found the third button at the beach yesterday, despite a lengthy search, and she'd given the dining and living rooms a good search last night as well. Priti loved those buttons, and Zoey needed all three. Where was that third button? Allie *had* said that it was perfect for a project she was working on.

"Marcus," Zoey said impulsively, "is there any chance Allie might have taken something from my sewing supplies when she was here the other day?"

Marcus looked horrified. He couldn't even answer.

Zoey immediately realized the implication of what she'd said. "Omigosh, that came out wrong! I don't mean that she *stole* it or anything, Marcus. She's my friend! I just mean, maybe she *borrowed* something for a project, planning to replace it, or put something in her pocket by mistake. Do you know if . . . if she did?"

Marcus smacked his hand on the kitchen table. "Jeez, Zoey, what's going on with you? You keep saying I'm distracted and all that, and you keep accusing me of not mailing your letter, and now you're accusing

Allie of *stealing* stuff from you?" He shook his head.

Quickly, Zoey apologized. "I'm so sorry, Marcus. I know I probably sound nuts. It's just that I haven't heard about my letter yet, and this really important button for Priti's new room has disappeared, and I don't know what's going on!"

Marcus stood up and took his cereal bowl to the sink to rinse and then put in the dishwasher. "Well, here's a tip—don't run around accusing people of stealing from you unless you're sure they did. Oh, and probably, your brother and your good friend aren't people who would do that, anyway! Sheesh."

Marcus stormed off, leaving Zoey alone at the kitchen table to think. What was happening to her judgment? Was she juggling too many projects at once? That could be. Not to mention she was awfully worried about both Kate and Priti at the moment, with everything they had going on. But that was no excuse for hurting her brother's feelings. Zoey loved being a designer, but she loved her friends and family more.

Zoey vowed to make it up to Marcus somehow. In the meantime she had a lot of sewing to do.

CHAPTER 7

Ready to *Fall* Over!

Ugh—I feel terrible! I just accused my brother and another person (who shall remain nameless) of doing two separate things that are so obviously ridiculous, I can't believe I even said the words! But for some reason I feel like a snowball running down a hill and growing out of control. There's been music coming from the basement (where my brother's band is practicing for their big audition for the Camp of Rock) all day, and it's making me batty. You can only listen to someone pounding on a drum set for maybe an hour . . . and I'm up to hour five!

Maybe I need a change of scene, and SCENERY, to feel better. . . . It's almost time to say good-bye to summer. I just sketched this gorgeous dress as a nod to fall. See the leaves? I'll need just the right fabrics to be able to pull it off, but this is going to be *cool.* If only I can get through these final (very loud) weeks of summer! HELP!

To escape the noise from the basement, not to mention her guilt from her earlier conversation with Marcus, Zoey decided to hide at Kate's house for the evening. It would give Marcus a chance to cool down, and Zoey hoped if she could sit somewhere *quiet* for a half an hour, she'd be able to think clearly again.

Mrs. Mackey ushered Zoey up to Kate's room,

and once Zoey was comfortable lounging on Kate's bed, enjoying the pleasant stillness of the Mackey house, she relaxed.

"It's sooooo nice here," she said to Kate. "You're lucky! Marcus's band has completely taken over our house. My dad's hiding at work—I'm sure of it. He's never gone all day on the weekends. We all support Marcus's band, and we want him to do well at his audition, but seriously! I'm starting to lose it!"

Kate giggled. She was perched at the top of her bed, sitting upright so her arm could rest properly. Her long blond hair poured down one shoulder, and on the other shoulder was one of the sling covers Zoey had made for her last spring, when she'd sprained her elbow. It reminded Zoey that she had another to-do-list item: make more slings for Kate.

"What's Marcus's band's name again?" Kate asked.

"The Space Invaders," said Zoey. "Isn't that funny? It's from some old video game."

Kate nodded. "What are they going to wear to the audition? They need to look perfect."

"That's a good question. Maybe I should offer

to . . ." Zoey's voice trailed off as an idea came to her. "That's it, Kate! I'll make them really awesome T-shirts to wear for their audition! Like those old, vintage band tees he loves, with the silk-screened logos, but more modern."

"*Great* idea!" said Kate. "Marcus will love it."

Zoey heaved a sigh of relief. "See? I just needed ten minutes of peace and quiet for my brain to start working properly again. Marcus will forgive me when I give him the shirts."

"Forgive you for what?" asked Kate.

"Oh, just something dumb I did," said Zoey. "You know me—sewing too hard, doing too much. I lost a few things and sort of flipped my lid."

"You? Doing too much? *Never*."

"Ha-ha, Mackey, very funny!"

Kate grinned. "Since you're here, and it's quiet, do you want to start working on the shirts? I'd love to help—even if it's just as your sounding board to bounce ideas off of. I feel like I have so much time now without swimming." Her voice caught on the word "swimming," and Zoey knew Kate was really having a hard time with her mandatory sports time-out.

Zoey was glad she was there to distract Kate.

"Yes!" said Zoey. "Let me grab my sketchbook . . ." She fished through her bag and pulled out her sketch- book and pencil. She flipped to a clean page and then gripped her pencil, poised to create.

Kate stared at her. "What's wrong? You're usu- ally sketching by now!"

Zoey blinked. She did have an idea for the shirts, but it was an image she wanted to draw and put *on* the shirts, not something she could just sew together. "I know—I just realized something. I want to draw a design and *print* it, not sew it. How can I do all that in time? They need the shirts in just a few days!"

Kate thought for a second and then picked up her laptop from the floor. "Leave that to me. You start working on the design and give me a few min- utes to research."

Zoey shrugged. "Okay—sounds good to me!"

Closing her eyes for a second, Zoey took sev- eral deep breaths. Since the Space Invaders name referred to a video game, she thought it would be neat to have an icon for the band that looked like graphics from an old video game. She started sketching little characters who were a mishmash of tiny robots and aliens, and kept at it until she had a few little guys she liked. She added a few flourishes and then sat back to look it over.

"I think I have something," Zoey said, holding the pad away from her body to study it from afar.

"Me too," said Kate. "Guess what you're going to do!"

Kate turned the laptop around and showed Zoey the listing for a class at the local college where Zoey's dad worked for the athletics department as a sports therapist.

"'Screen-printing class'?" Zoey read. "Of course!" She scanned the listing for the class and saw that it was open to ages twelve and up. It met weeknight evenings on campus. Students brought their own T-shirts to use and could pay by the class. Zoey could start immediately, and hopefully, get the shirts completed in the next few days! All she had to do was get her father's permission and the money to attend the classes, which she had saved up, thanks to her number-one Etsy customer, Dakota Brown. "This is awesome, Kate, thank you!"

Kate smiled, looking pleased to be so helpful. "I'm glad it's going to work out! I think Marcus will *love* the shirts, and it'll give his whole band confidence for their audition."

Zoey picked up her bag again to look for her phone. Then she sent a text message to her father that she was hiding at Kate's house while Marcus's band finished, and could she please take a screenprinting class the following week?

He texted back, **Yes, of course!** And **Band shuts down at 7 p.m. Come home and see your old dad.**

Zoey laughed and returned the phone to her bag. "Dad's going to kick the band out in another hour or so. Can I stay here until then?"

Kate nodded. "Of course! Stay for dinner. We're having chicken cacciatore."

"Yum!" said Zoey. "I'm staying! Let's look through your closet for a first-day-of-school outfit. I'm going to need to make you a sling to go with it, so I need to know what you'll be wearing."

"I'd *like* to be wearing my swim team warm-ups," Kate admitted.

"I know," said Zoey. "Any word from your doctor

or your coach about when you might be cleared to swim again?"

Kate shook her head. "No; they've said I'm doing a good job resting it, but they really don't want me to push myself. I'm still benched for a while."

"I'm sorry," said Zoey. "You're such a great swimmer, Kate. When you're all healed and ready, you'll be better than ever, I'm sure of it!"

Kate smiled ruefully. "I hope so. But until then, I might as well let you dress me like a mannequin. Go ahead, search my closet! You'll have a hard time finding anything more interesting than T-shirts and jeans. . . ."

"That's okay," said Zoey, her eyes twinkling. "Because I can always *make* you something more interesting. . . ."

On Sunday morning Zoey was up early and working. She had told the Flynns she'd have Sophie's dress cut and pinned together by lunchtime, so they could come over and have a fitting for Sophie.

She'd brought the dress and all her supplies home from Lulu's on Friday and had everything spread out on the dining room table as she worked. She liked to be able to see all her supplies, so she knew what she had to work with and what she still needed to finish.

Immediately, she noticed a swatch of fabric she'd earmarked for a throw pillow in Priti's room was missing. She searched her bag for it, twice, with no success. It wasn't a total crisis, because she had the corresponding bolt of fabric she needed to *make* the pillow, but she liked to keep swatches for creating mood boards and concept boards, or just to tote around with her, in case she needed them for reference.

Zoey shook her head, frustrated that another item from Priti's project had disappeared.

At least Sophie's dress is coming together nicely, Zoey thought. The fabric-blocking design she'd come up with was really cute. She hoped Sophie would like it as much as she did!

Marcus's band was at it again in the basement, so Zoey put in her headphones and listened to music while she worked. When Sophie, Libby, and Mrs. Flynn arrived, they had to really bang on the front door for Zoey to hear them. She pulled out the head-phones from her ears and then ran to open the door.

"Hi, guys," she yelled over the music. "Sorry about the noise. My brother's band has a *huge* audition coming up, and they've been practicing nonstop."

Mrs. Flynn looked alarmed by the pounding of the drums in the basement. Zoey could almost see her temples throbbing.

"I guess you get used to it, right?" Mrs. Flynn asked.

Zoey shook her head. "No, not really."

In the living room, Zoey ushered Sophie to the couch and told her to close her eyes. Then she went and got the pinned-together dress from where it was hidden in the dining room and brought it over to show her.

"Here it is!" Zoey cried, excited to show off her creation.

Sophie's eyes flew open and she clapped her hands and squealed. "I *love* it!!" she declared. "It is the most *beautiful* dress in the entire world! I'll never take it off!"

Zoey, Libby, and Mrs. Flynn laughed.

"Well, eventually, we'll have to wash it," said Mrs. Flynn. "But I'm glad you're so happy, Sophie! I think it's beautiful too. What a wonderful job you're doing, Zoey."

Mrs. Flynn beamed at her, and Zoey smiled back. This was her favorite part of being a designer—getting to see happy customers as they tried on their new outfits.

Sophie carefully put on the dress and modeled it for everyone.

Libby looked really pleased and clapped her hands together. "You look *great*, Soph!"

Sophie did a little dance in her dress, as if to show how happy it made her and how well she could move in it. "I can do monkey bars in it!" Sophie exclaimed.

Libby caught Zoey's eye, and they both smiled.

Zoey turned Sophie around a few times to study the dress from different angles. "I think it needs just a few alterations. Come into the dining room with me, Sophie, where my pins are. I'm going to make some adjustments, okay?"

The whole crew followed Zoey and Sophie, and oohed and ahhed when they saw Zoey's worktable, laid out with rows and rows of swatches and accessories.

"It's almost like you have your own fabric store in here," Libby joked.

Zoey laughed. "Well, I'm in the middle of a bunch of different projects, and I'm going to try to make Kate a sling later today, so I've got to keep all my stuff organized or I'll never finish everything. It's a good thing my dad and brother don't mind eating in the kitchen all the time!"

Zoey re-pinned Sophie's dress and wrote down a few notes. Even though she'd just measured her a week ago, the dress looked like it was a little short—shorter than Zoey had intended it to be. There was time to fix it, though, and plenty of extra material.

"I'll have it done and perfect this week," Zoey promised.

Sophie nodded happily, her eyes shining with pleasure about her new dress. "Can we stay here for a while, Mom?" she asked Mrs. Flynn. "I love looking at all of Zoey's design stuff!"

"You can look for a minute, okay? I want to talk to Zoey." Mrs. Flynn nodded her head at Zoey and Libby, indicating the three of them should step back into the living room to talk.

Zoey and Libby obeyed, leaving Sophie in the dining room, where she wouldn't be able to over-hear them. "Is everything okay?" Zoey asked.

Mrs. Flynn quickly waved a hand. "Oh yes, of course! Sorry if I worried you. I just want to thank you again, privately, for making this special dress for Sophie. She hasn't stopped talking about it, or *you*, since we went to the Cody Calloway concert. I know this might sound odd, but Libby and I think you've been a really good influence on her!"

Zoey couldn't help blushing. She was happy to be someone's good influence! And just by doing what came natural to her—sewing. She looked at Libby, who reached over and squeezed her hand.

"There's no need to thank me," Zoey said modestly. "I love making clothes for people!"

Just then, Sophie tiptoed into the room and peered around Libby. "Mom, can we please stay for longer than one minute?"

Mrs. Flynn grimaced, as there was a deafening crescendo from the music coming from the basement. "Um, not today, honey. We've got to get Libby to her dance rehearsal, remember? But we'll come back another day, all right?"

Zoey looked at Libby as she picked up her headphones once again. "Take me with you?" she joked. "Please?"

Libby smiled. "I wish we could."

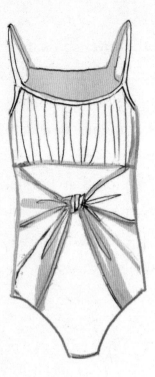

------- CHAPTER 8 -------

DYEing to Try Screen Printing!!

I am very, very excited! I'm trying something totally new tonight—screen printing! (Get it? *Dyeing?*) My friend Kate found me this class where I can learn to print designs onto clothing. I've come up with a pretty neat design for a SPECIAL PROJECT for a FAMILY MEMBER who probably isn't reading this blog, because he's way too busy putting cracks in our house by turning the bass way up on his band's speakers. (Really, there's a crack on the wall of the kitchen, and my dad thinks it's from M's band practicing!) I can't post the sketch of that project here, just in case you-know-who sees it, so I've posted another one of some leg warmers and a leotard I'm going to make for my friend Libby (someday, when I have more time), who has been busy-busy at ballet camp this summer and had to miss our fun beach day this past Friday.

A few readers have posted and asked if I've heard from Fashionsista yet—and the answer is no. But I DO have confirmation that my letter was mailed. Fashionsista—are you out there?! Hello?

Zoey went to Camp Lulu on Monday, ready to switch gears and dedicate herself to working on Project Priti for the day. She brought all her materials with her, as usual, because she never knew exactly when or on what part of the project she'd be in the mood to work on. Luckily, Lulu had a sewing machine for Zoey to use, so she didn't have to lug that along as well!

Lulu was home for the morning, with no client appointments, so she and Zoey went over the details of the project. Lulu had been very helpful by keeping Zoey on track with such a large job.

"This is the fabric Priti liked for the pillows and duvet," Zoey said, showing them to her aunt. "And I think I'm going to do them first, since they're so easy to sew, and it'll make me feel like I've accomplished a lot."

Lulu nodded. "Good. I like that plan, Zoey. And I have terrific news to share: I talked to Mr. Holbrooke yesterday, and he agreed to order all the new furniture pieces I selected, as well as some picture frames, lamps, and a mirror! The new pieces will really make your pillows and duvet and fabric-covered bulletin board pop."

Zoey clapped. "Aunt Lulu! That's great! Priti thinks we'll just be dressing up some old bed frame and dresser from the attic in her mom's house. I know new furniture will make her so happy. She gets so many hand-me-downs from her older sisters!"

Aunt Lulu chuckled. "That's what I thought. Mr. Holbrooke is anxious to make Priti feel happy and comfortable in his new apartment."

"Maybe it's a good time for Priti to ask for a new laptop then, too," Zoey quipped.

"Maybe it is," Aunt Lulu said.

Lulu's cell phone rang, and she answered it right away, mumbling "Helllllo" and taking the phone into her office for privacy. Zoey knew "helllllo" meant she was talking to John and that things must still be going very, very well between them.

Zoey smiled to herself, glad her aunt was happy and that so far, it hadn't affected Zoey's special relationship with her.

Alone, with heaps of work to do, Zoey got down to business. She started pulling accessories out of her bag and lining them up on the table. When she pulled out the sparkly ribbon she'd earmarked as piping for one of Priti's pillows, she decided to go ahead and tack it around the edge of the pillow fabric with straight pins, so she'd be ready to sew it when the duvet was done. She did the tacking roughly, not bothering to measure and line it up perfectly, but even so, the ribbon barely made it around the third side of the pillow.

Zoey studied the ribbon, unpinned it, and tried it again. It made no sense—it was still too short! She could have sworn she'd bought too *much* ribbon, because she'd been so sure Priti would love its sparkle and want to use it in several places. And now she didn't have enough for one pillow? Had she cut it and left the other half at home?

Zoey tried to retrace her steps. She'd had the ribbon at the beach, at home, and at Lulu's. She did not remember cutting it or starting to use it or doing something with the extra.

"I know I'm not the most organized person ever," Zoey muttered to herself, "but this is *ridiculous*. All of my things are disappearing! The button, the pillow fabric swatch, this ribbon. It's like I have my own personal cat burglar!"

At the word "cat," an idea struck Zoey. She didn't have a cat, but Aunt Lulu did have a dog, appropriately named Buttons. Was it possible Buttons was the thief? She had seen him eat live bugs outside, not to mention chew on Aunt Lulu's shoes and, once, one of her favorite purses.

Zoey went to look for Buttons, who she found curled up on his dog bed in the kitchen, contentedly chewing a dog bone. He didn't look guilty, but as she watched him methodically chew through the bone, she started to wonder.

Aunt Lulu came out of her office, pink-faced and smiling from her phone call. "Where were we?" she asked Zoey, who had returned to her sewing table and was sitting and staring at her things.

"Aunt Lulu," Zoey said, "is it possible Buttons could be eating my supplies? I'm missing a button and some ribbon, a swatch, and who knows what else. But I'm positive about how much stuff I bought, and now some of it is missing!"

Aunt Lulu frowned. "Hmm," she said. "I don't think so, but let's go look at him."

Lulu and Zoey went to the kitchen where Buttons had stopped chewing the bone and had fallen asleep with it between his front paws.

"Well, Zoey," Lulu said, "I think he looks too happy and comfortable to be the culprit. I'm not saying he *definitely* didn't eat your things, because he is a dog, but if he'd ingested ribbon and a button and a swatch, he'd been in pain, and his tummy would be hurting. I can keep an eye on him if you like, and I'll certainly make sure to check his . . . his *business* . . . to see if anything comes out. But I doubt it."

Zoey sighed. She really seemed to be blaming everyone lately for what was probably her own carelessness. Allie, Marcus, Buttons. Who would be next? Her father? The mailman? She knew she shouldn't be pointing fingers all the time. It wasn't right. And if she thought about things logically, the most *likely* reason things were missing was that she herself had misplaced them.

Maybe what she needed to do was just hurry up and finish her projects, before she lost anything else!

That evening Zoey dressed carefully for her screen-printing class. She knew printing might be messy, but she wanted to look nice, since some of the students could be young designers like herself. So she chose a pair of skinny camo pants and paired them with a printed cotton blouse, with differently colored polka dots that reminded her of a painter's palette. She loved the two patterns together—camo and polka dots. She carefully braided her long hair into a fishtail side braid and then added barrettes that had been her mother's at the top. Her father had offered to drive her back and forth to class the first night and said he and Marcus would split the driving the other nights.

Zoey was slightly nervous walking into the room, because, ordinarily, when she went somewhere new, especially somewhere like a class, she had a friend with her. Even at sleepaway camp she'd been with Priti. But she wouldn't know anyone at screen printing, and it was possible she'd be the youngest person there as well. She'd asked Kate if she'd want to come along for fun, but Kate declined, since her sling meant she wouldn't be able to participate fully.

It took Zoey a while to find the studio, but she managed to sneak in just as the teacher was closing the door. He was young, probably in his twenties, and looked like he might be a graduate student. From his paint-spattered clothes, blue-tinted fingertips, and long, messy ponytail, Zoey got the feeling he was someone who lived to make art and that he'd probably be a lot of fun in class.

The room was nearly full, mostly with high school kids and college students, but Zoey spotted one empty seat on the left side of the art studio, near the back. She headed toward it and plopped her bag down onto the floor. She climbed onto the stool and folded her hands on the table in front of her. She was eager and excited to get started. She'd polished her design for the Space Invaders T-shirt until she felt it was perfect, and now she was anxious to see it on a shirt.

The teacher introduced himself and started talking. The person next to Zoey took a handout from a stack of papers being passed around, and gave one to her.

"Here, Zoey," she whispered.

Startled, Zoey looked over at the person, wondering how they knew her name. It was Shannon Chang!

"Hi, Shannon," Zoey said automatically. She bit her lip. For the past year or so, it had been hard to know which Shannon she was talking to at any given time. There was Old Shannon, who had been Zoey's friend in elementary school, and New Shannon, who hung around with mean girls Ivy and Bree at school and watched silently as they spat insults at Zoey and her friends.

Zoey didn't like to be around mean people, but she couldn't bring herself to be rude in return by ignoring them. She just wasn't made like that. She was friendly, and she was herself.

"So what are you doing at screen-printing class?" she asked Shannon, as if they saw each other all the time and got along perfectly well.

"I've been taking it for a few weeks," Shannon said. "I really got into art last year, and my parents thought I should try a few different mediums to see what I liked."

Zoey wanted to ask where Ivy and Bree were, but didn't. There was no need to mention them if Shannon was going to be friendly. Zoey and Shannon weren't at school, anyway. They were on neutral territory.

"Are you here to work on those T-shirts for Marcus?" Shannon asked. "I was wondering if you'd find this class."

"How'd you know about that?" Zoey asked, alarmed.

Shannon blushed. "I read your blog sometimes, and I guessed the 'family member' was your brother. I like your blog—your sketches are so neat. I really love it when you post an early sketch of something, and then the final sketch later, after you've changed the design. It's so cool to see the process."

Zoey couldn't help feeling flattered. It was always nice to hear that someone liked her work and read about it.

"Thank you," said Zoey, pulling out her sketch for the band shirts. "This is the design I made for Marcus, and I've got to make four or five really good shirts by this weekend! Do you think I can do it?"

Shannon looked impressed by the design. "I love it! And, yes, you can do it. I'll help you. I've made a bunch of stuff already, so I sort of know what I'm doing. Don't worry—we'll get them done in time."

Zoey smiled gratefully at Shannon, and Shannon smiled back.

Zoey was very, very glad she'd decided to sign up for screen-printing class.

--------- CHAPTER 9 ---------

Coming Out of the Cocoon . . .

Wow, just WOW. I went to a screen-printing class last night and felt SEW inspired being around all those awesome people bringing their beautiful designs to life! I sketched this tunic shirt because the shape reminded me of a butterfly. Doesn't it look pretty? I have to figure out how much material it will take, though. I'd like to find a great, colorful fabric that reminds me of butterfly wings, and all the yardage will probably be expensive. So if any of you are thinking of buying something from my Etsy site, now would be a good time! ☺

It's funny how butterflies start off as caterpillars, and they look like furry worms, but then they go into their cocoons and come out looking completely different and are able to fly! So even when something (or someONE, and I'm thinking of a certain person here . . .) looks or acts one way on the outside, they can be something completely different on the inside.

In other news, I've been losing sewing supplies. ☹ It's the weirdest thing—it seems like every time I sit down to work, I notice a swatch or button is missing from my bag. I've decided I have a personal fashion burglar! Either that, or I'm continually losing things because I carry around so much stuff! But even with all the missing stuff, I'm still having a blast finishing up the design for Priti's room and making my secret project for my family member (shh!). Tackling new types of design work and using different mediums has turned out to be so much fun! I can't wait to wake up every morning and figure out what I'm going to be doing. Maybe I'm learning to fly, just like a butterfly!!

Zoey went down to breakfast on Tuesday to find a small pharmacy bag at her spot at the kitchen table. Someone had written "Zoey" on the bag in marker.

"A present?" Zoey said to herself. "For me?"

Her father came into the kitchen with his travel coffee mug, ready to fill it up and head out to work. "What's that, Zoey?" he asked.

"Did you leave this bag?" Zoey asked him.

Her father bit his lip to conceal a smile and shook his head. "No, I'm afraid not. It's from Marcus, and I got one as well. Don't get your hopes up too high that it's something you're really going to like."

Zoey furrowed her brow, unsure of what could possibly be in the bag. When she opened it, she found a pair of earplugs, with a note from Marcus that read:

Sorry. Just four more days until the audition Saturday! ☺

Zoey sighed. "I guess that means they'll be practicing all day today, too?"

Her father nodded. "Yep. At least you'll be at Lulu's, right? I might be staying late at work."

Zoey frowned. She'd been planning to sew at home that day, because Aunt Lulu had a client coming to her house for an appointment, and Zoey didn't like to be underfoot when her aunt had someone there.

Marcus strolled into the kitchen and grabbed a bagel to put in the toaster. "I see you got your gift, Zoey," he teased. "Want me to put in a bagel for you?"

"Yes, please," said Zoey. "And, yes, I got my *gift*. I'm beginning to wish I'd never given you that flyer about band camp."

Marcus grinned. "C'mon now, loving sister. You don't mean that!"

Zoey scowled but couldn't hold it, and the scowl slid into a smile. Marcus's grin was just too big for her to really be mad. She was proud of Marcus, and she could tell how much the band was improving from all the practice.

The toaster dinged, and Marcus spread cream cheese on both bagels. He placed them on the kitchen table and then sat down across from Zoey.

"Thanks for the bagel," she said. "I guess I can listen to your band for a *few* more days."

"Thanks, Zo." Marcus chewed for a moment. Then he said, "You know, with all the practicing we've been doing, I've hardly been able to see Allie at all. I keep asking her to come over and watch us, but she's so busy finishing up pieces for her Etsy site. She can never come over. Do you know if something's going on with her?"

Zoey could hear the sadness in Marcus's voice. He wanted Allie there to support him, and so he could see her, but at the same time, they were both so busy.

"Don't worry, Marcus—there's nothing going on that I know about. I'm sure she'll come by soon. And it's not like you can really hang out with her when you're practicing, anyway! Just call her later and tell her you miss her. I'm sure she'd like to hear that. And tell her you hope all her projects are going well."

"You think so?" said Marcus. "That's all it is?"

"I *know* so," said Zoey. "Just call her."

"Okay, okay."

There was a knock on the front door.

"That's the band," Marcus said, jumping up to answer the door. "Time to put in the earplugs, Zo!"

Zoey sighed. "Okay. Yeesh."

The earplugs helped slightly, but not much. Zoey ended up dragging her sewing machine from the dining room up to her bedroom. With her door shut and her bathrobe rolled up as extra soundproofing along the bottom of the doorframe, the room was somewhat quieter.

Before she got down to work, Zoey picked up her phone and called Allie.

Allie answered right away. "Hi, Zoey!" she said cheerily, obviously happy to hear from her. "How are all your projects going?"

"Pretty well," Zoey said. "I'm busy, though. I started a screen-printing class, and I really love it."

"Oh wow!" said Allie. "I've always wanted to do that. Maybe I can go with you sometime!"

"That'd be great!" said Zoey. "I'm making something special for Marcus there—T-shirts for his band to wear to the audition."

"Oooh, that's awesome—he's going to love them," Allie said. "I finally came up with an idea for the band, too. I'm in the middle of making them leather cuffs to wear, so they'll look really rock 'n' roll."

Zoey loved the idea and loved Allie even more for doing something so nice for her brother. "That's great, Allie! I know Marcus will like them."

"Oh good—phew." Allie sounded pleased. "He's been sort of upset with me that I haven't been able to come over, but I'm working on two new items for my site, and now I'm making the cuffs, and I'm thinking of adding them as an item on my site too. I just haven't been able to come over this week!"

As Allie talked about her projects and Marcus, Zoey began to realize how silly she had been to ever think Allie would have borrowed supplies from her without asking. She was her *friend* and her brother's girlfriend. It just seemed completely out of character for her to take another designer's supplies, especially when she knew how important they were! It was much *more* likely, Zoey thought, that she herself had been careless and was losing stuff because she was overwhelmed by too many things to do. She was glad she'd never said anything directly to Allie and risked their friendship.

The girls talked a bit longer about their different projects, and when they were done, Zoey asked Allie to please come over as soon as possible.

"Not just to visit Marcus, but to visit me too!" Zoey said. "I miss you."

"Me too," said Allie. "And don't worry, I'll see you *very* soon!"

Zoey got off the phone, made sure her earplugs were firmly in place, and turned on her sewing machine.

Zoey continued to go to screen-printing class, and by the third night, she'd made some real progress on the shirts. She was happy with the stencil she'd created, and to make each shirt slightly different, she was using different inks for each person in the band. Her plan was to make a bunch of shirts and choose the best ones to give to the band. When the shirts were all printed, she planned to give them a special Sew Zoey twist: She was going to cut out duplicate images of the little characters on the shirts and then sew them on top of the images on each shirt, to give the designs texture and to make them stand out. She couldn't wait to see what they'd look like when she was finished.

As she was coming out of class one night, her arms full of the shirts that were finished and dry, she ran smack into her friend Gabe Monaco from school.

"Gabe, what are you doing here?" Zoey exclaimed.

Gabe grinned. "Hi, Zoey! I'm taking a photography class. What are *you* doing? Laundry?"

"Ha-ha." Zoey laughed, and explained about the screen-printing class and making the shirts for her brother's band.

"Wow—that's so cool. I heard about the concert they're having for the end of the Camp of Rock week," Gabe said. "It's supposed to have an awesome guest rock band!"

Zoey nodded. "That's what I heard. I just hope my brother's band will be there too!"

"I'm sure he will be. I've already got tickets for the show."

"How's your photography class?" Zoey asked. She didn't know much about photography, but she'd always found it interesting. Maybe one day she'd take a class herself.

"Oh man, it's awesome. I'm learning so much stuff! If you ever need someone with crazy-good photography skills, call me. I'm really getting into it, and my parents said if I keep it up, they might get me a nice camera for Christmas."

Zoey smiled. "That's so neat! You know, I might need your help sometime. I'm terrible at taking pictures of my pieces for my clothing site. Marcus used to help me, but he's been so busy lately—first, with his girlfriend, and now, with the band. Maybe you could help instead!"

"I'd love to!" Gabe said. "I still owe you for the outfit you made my dog, Mr. Paws."

Zoey laughed. She'd almost forgotten the name of Gabe's dog. She knew Gabe had to be a nice guy if he was willing to admit in public that he'd named his dog Mr. Paws.

"Well, I've got to go meet my dad," Zoey said. "I'll see you around!" She waved good-bye to Gabe and headed outside to find her father's car.

The next day Zoey was pleased to learn Aunt Lulu had no clients coming to the house, so Zoey would be able to camp out there for the day and avoid the Space Invaders's never-ending practice sessions. If it went on much longer, she was going to suggest to Marcus they rename the band the Noisy Invaders; the Never-Ending Invaders; or the Nonstop, Noisy, Never-Ending Invaders. She didn't think Marcus would find it funny, but she no longer found having to avoid her own house all day, every day, very funny, either. As much as she loved and supported her brother, she couldn't help wishing his band would find somewhere else to practice!

At Lulu's, she set up in the dining room, as per usual, and was relieved to find that for once, all the items she'd *thought* she'd packed seemed to actually be there. There was just one thing she needed to borrow from Lulu.

"Aunt Lulu?" she said.

Aunt Lulu was dressed and sitting on the sofa, finishing her coffee and skimming through a clipboard of invoices. "Yes, dear?"

"Do you, by any chance, have a zipper or two or three I could borrow? The nice kind you use on pillows?"

Zoey had had an idea for how to make sure the dress she'd nearly completed for Sophie would last a bit longer than just September and October, and she was anxious to get it finished. She wanted to deliver it to Mrs. Flynn as soon as possible.

"Well, sure, I probably have a few," said Aunt Lulu. "For Priti's pillowcases? I thought you'd finished those."

Zoey shook her head. "No, actually I'm thinking of adding more fabric blocks to the bottom of Sophie's dress and having them zip on by hiding the zipper up under the hem of the original bottom panel. That way, if the dress starts to get too short too soon, Mrs. Flynn can zip on another few inches of fabric, and no one will know!"

Aunt Lulu looked impressed. "Zoey, what a terrific idea! And more panels of fabric will just make it even cuter. I can't wait to see it! Let me go get you some zippers . . ."

Lulu hopped up and headed into her office. Zoey heard some rustling, then a phone ringing and being answered, and then a few minutes later, her aunt emerged from the office, looking serious.

Zoey immediately assumed Lulu had gotten a phone call with bad news from someone. Perhaps an unhappy client?

"Aunt Lulu, what's the matter?"

Lulu came into the dining room, carrying one of her upholstery fabric books instead of a zipper. She placed the book on the table beside Zoey's work space.

"What is the book for?" Zoey asked.

Aunt Lulu looked like she was in pain. "I just got a call from a client, so I had to check for a sample of something I could show her later today, and when I opened up this book to see the sample, I found this."

Lulu opened the book to reveal a page with a fabric sample on it, except a large, rough circle of fabric had been cut out of the sample.

"I hate to even ask you this, Zoey, but did you cut this out and forget to ask me about it first? Because this is one of my newer books and not one I've ever cut something from."

Zoey was horrified. She couldn't believe what she was seeing. Or hearing. "Of course it wasn't me, Aunt Lulu! I promise. I would *never* cut something from one of your beautiful books. I know how important they are!"

Lulu closed the book and sat down, nodding. "Of course, of course. I'm so sorry I even asked, Zoey. It's just such an odd thing to find. And I need to use this very sample later to show a client. . . ."

"That's so *weird*," Zoey said. "I mean, I've had so many things missing recently, and now you have a random piece cut out from the middle of your book!"

Aunt Lulu laughed. "If only there were aliens. That would explain everything."

"But it really is strange," Zoey insisted. "I've been driving myself nuts trying to figure out where my buttons and swatches and ribbons have been going. I thought I had my own personal fashion burglar, but now you do too!"

Aunt Lulu shrugged. "I'm sure there's some reasonable explanation. I lose buttons and things for projects all the time. Probably because I haul things from my house to my car to clients' houses, and back. Things are bound to go missing. I probably took this book to visit someone last week, and while I was in the restroom, they decided they liked this sample and wanted to keep it."

Zoey thought hard. She wished she could be as calm about her missing items. "Aunt Lulu, I almost accused my friend Allie of taking some of my supplies," Zoey confessed. "That's how nutty it's made me."

"Well, I'm glad you didn't!" Aunt Lulu said. "I seriously doubt it was Allie. Just like I doubted you'd done this, and I'm terribly sorry I even asked you. Forgive me?"

"Of course!" said Zoey. "It sure is strange, though, isn't it?"

"Very," agreed Aunt Lulu. "And now I'm off to the store to get another sample for this client. I'm dying to know how Sophie's dress turns out. Will you show it to me later?"

----------- CHAPTER 10 -----------

Nancy Drew, Where Are You?

I've got a mystery to solve! My "fashion burglar" has grown even more, well, mysterious! My aunt Lulu found a chunk of fabric cut out from one of her sample books. Are there sneaky, magical mice running around, making a dress for Cinderella from all the scraps? I can't figure it out! If I only I knew a real, live detective . . .

Marcus's band continues to practice (and improve, thankfully!), and his big audition is tomorrow. If they're accepted into camp, the Space Invaders will play ON THE BEACH next weekend! How neat is that? I'm SO hoping they'll make it (for many reasons), because I sketched this adorable rock 'n' roll–inspired beach outfit to wear to the performance. Do you like it? I need to hurry up and start sewing to have it ready for next weekend. But first the band needs to rock their audition!

One of my loyal readers commented the other day and asked if I'd heard back yet from Fashionsista, and I'm sorry to tell you the answer is STILL NO. I'm starting to think I invented the whole thing! Or is Fashionsista yet another mystery I can't solve?

Since it was the Space Invaders' last day of practice before their live audition, Allie came over to watch Marcus and support the band. Zoey was up in her room when Allie arrived, but she could hear Allie and Marcus talking and was pleased by how happy they both sounded to see each other.

Zoey had finally finished the T-shirts for the members of the band, and she couldn't wait to show them to everyone. The screen-printed pieces that Zoey had hand-sewn on, slightly askew, over the little Space Invaders characters had turned out terrific, and she knew the band would look both modern and retro in their shirts. She hoped it would help them make the perfect impression on the judges.

She gathered up the shirts and headed downstairs, excited to give the band their gifts. Since it was their last day of practicing in the basement for a while, Zoey was already forgetting the headaches of the past week.

When she reached the bottom of the stairs, she placed the neatly folded shirts on a table and motioned to the band to stop playing.

Marcus obeyed but looked perplexed at why she was cutting them off midsong. "What is it, Zo?" he asked, silencing the cymbal on his drum kit.

Excitedly, Zoey held up one of the shirts. "Surprise! I made you guys shirts to wear to your audition tomorrow! Come look."

Looking pleased, Marcus came over to examine

the shirts. As he did, Zoey leaned in close to him and whispered, "I'm so sorry about being a jerk about the letter and my missing stuff. Forgive me?"

Marcus, who was grinning from ear to ear as he held up his custom Space Invaders T-shirt, just laughed. "Sure, Zoey. And I'm sorry *I* was kind of a jerk, and that we were so loud all week."

Dan, the band's guitar player, pulled on one of the shirts and said, "Wow, Zoey! I can't believe you made these! We look so legit now. Thanks!"

Marcus pulled one over his head as well. "These are *awesome*! You're the best, Zoey!"

Zoey watched as Ralph, the lead singer, pulled on a shirt. They looked terrific all together like that, especially since each shirt's design and fabrics were a little bit different.

Thrilled her surprise had been such a hit, Zoey decided to sit and listen to a song before getting back to work. She went over to sit beside Allie, who was parked on the couch knitting something for her accessories line. Zoey expected Allie to look happy that Marcus and his band loved their shirts so much, but instead Allie looked like she was about to cry, and wouldn't meet Zoey's eyes.

The band started to play again, and Zoey nervously turned to Allie. "What's wrong?" she asked. "You don't like the shirts?"

Allie shook her head. "No, that's not it. They look amazing. You know they do. But I haven't given the leather cuffs to the boys yet, because I wanted to do it tomorrow, right before their audition—for good luck."

Zoey was confused. "Okay . . . but I don't understand. You still can!"

Allie frowned. "Yeah, but now they've already gotten an awesome surprise gift for the auditions, so mine won't seem as exciting." Allie sighed. "I'm sorry—I know I sound like such a grump. It's just that I've been feeling so badly about not being here for Marcus all week, and I really wanted to show him how much I support him. And I thought the surprise would do that. But a *second* surprise is never as good as the first surprise."

Zoey understood. She'd felt badly about yelling at Marcus and wanted to make it up to him with the T-shirts, and she knew Allie wanted to make up for missing time with Marcus by giving him the cuffs. It felt good to give someone a special gift you'd planned, and worked hard on, but then to be trumped by another person's gift just beforehand, on top of already feeling guilty, must be extra tough.

"I'm so sorry, Allie," Zoey said. "I just didn't think! I was so excited about the shirts that I sort of forgot about everything else. I really didn't mean to upset you or get in the way of your gift."

The girls were so busy talking, they hadn't even noticed the band had stopped playing. Marcus was standing right in front of them.

"Hey, what's wrong? Why are you two looking so sad? We're going to make it tomorrow, I know it!"

Zoey quickly explained the situation, and Marcus caught on. He grabbed Allie's hand and held it tightly. "Hey, we're going to love your surprise tomorrow—whatever it is. Two surprises are always better than one! I can't wait to see what you made for us."

After a minute or two more of convincing, Allie finally smiled. Marcus whispered something in her ear and then went back to stand with his band.

"This song is for you, Allie," he said into the microphone.

He picked up his new guitar and started playing acoustically, and singing a very unrock song just to her.

Zoey noticed Marcus's band rolling their eyes, smiling, as if wanting to tease Marcus for so obviously adoring his girlfriend. But they didn't say anything, and neither did Zoey. Maybe a little part of her wanted to groan at how corny it was, but the rest of her was glad Marcus and Allie were happy again. She stayed and listened to the band for a while and took a few pictures of them with her phone to send to her father and Aunt Lulu.

The next afternoon Zoey got a text and a picture from Marcus of the Space Invaders at the audition. They were wearing the T-shirts and leather cuffs, and they all had huge smiles on their faces. The text read, **We made it!**

Zoey texted back, **Congrats! U deserve it!!!!**

Judges loved the shirts, he wrote back. Then, **Thx, Zo.**

Zoey smiled. Her brother's band had made it into rock camp. Who knew what amazing things they'd learn there or how far their band would go? And to think, it was really Cody Calloway who helped Marcus end up at rock camp, because that's the concert Zoey was attending when she saw the flyer!

She resisted the urge to tell her brother that, and instead wrote back, **Anytime, big brother.**

On Monday, with Marcus's band gone for the day at rock camp, Zoey decided to spend the day working at home instead of at Lulu's, to finish up the accessories for Priti's room. At five o'clock, she was still wearing pajama pants and had only eaten a peanut butter sandwich all day. She decided she needed to get out of the house. She wanted to check on Kate, to see how her shoulder was doing, so she threw on a pair of leggings but left her messy T-shirt and ponytail in place. After all, Kate wouldn't mind, and Zoey only needed to look presentable enough to walk up the block.

As she was about to leave, she yelled good-bye to

her father, who'd come home from work early since the band was no longer practicing at the house.

"Wait, Zoey, where are you going?" Mr. Webber asked, sounding concerned.

Zoey had her hand on the front doorknob, puzzled. "Just up to Kate's for a while. I've been home all day. Why?"

Mr. Webber looked nervous. "Uh, well, I haven't seen you much lately. Could you stay home and have dinner with me?"

"I'll come home for dinner. It's only five. What's going on, Dad?"

Then Marcus came downstairs. He'd just gotten back from rock camp and had immediately hopped in the shower. Now, wearing his band T-shirt, with his damp hair neatly combed, he glanced at his father and at Zoey, who was still standing by the front door.

"You should go clean yourself up," Marcus told Zoey. "We can have a nice dinner with Dad tonight."

"'Clean myself up'?" she repeated. "Is it someone's birthday? What am I missing?"

Marcus shrugged innocently. "Nothing. I just

think maybe you should be dressed more like you usually are, in a Sew Zoey outfit or something."

"But *why*?"

With a groan, Marcus gave up. "All right, all right—jeez. There's a surprise coming, and I'm not telling you who it is, but you're going to want to look nice, okay?"

Zoey's heart started pounding. A surprise? Who could it be? Her mind went into overdrive. Could it be a visit from *Fashionsista*? Had she written to Zoey's dad instead of Zoey? Why else would Marcus tell her to wear a nice outfit?

Zoey quickly agreed to change and ran up to her room, texting the change of plans to Kate. She dug through a pile of clothes on her chair until she found a cute shirtdress she'd made recently, and a belt to wear with it. There wasn't time to do much with her hair, other than to brush it out and braid it neatly down one side. She slipped on a Sew Zoey fabric headband to make it a little more interesting. Just as she'd gotten her hair looking decent, the doorbell rang.

Was it Fashionsista?

Zoey flew back down the steps, running straight toward the front door.

"You get it, Zoey," her father called from the kitchen. Zoey could smell beef and onions cooking on the stove. "Marcus is in the basement."

Zoey reached the door and threw it open. Simultaneously, her jaw dropped, her palms started sweating, and her heart began to pound. She couldn't believe who she was seeing.

Cody Calloway was on her front doorstep!

Cody wore a leather jacket over a T-shirt and jeans. He looked like he'd just stepped out of the pages of one of her teen magazines. His teeth gleamed white, and his smile was a mile wide. His dirty blond hair was thick and pushed over to one side.

"You must be Zoey," he said.

He held out his hand to Zoey, and she shook it numbly. His hand was warm and soft, and it made her knees turn to jelly.

"Uhh-umm," she sputtered. "Hiii."

He moved toward her slightly. As he did, Zoey saw a girl behind him who looked about her age.

And she was wearing a Sew Zoey shirt!

"What's going on?" Zoey managed to ask. "How did you get that shirt? And *what* are you doing here?"

"Marcus didn't tell you?" Cody asked, confused.

"You know my *brother*?"

Cody started to laugh, and from behind Zoey, Marcus appeared. "Hey, man," Marcus said to Cody, slapping him a high-five. "C'mon in."

Cody and the girl came *inside Zoey's house*, and all Zoey could do was stare. Cody Calloway was in her house, acting like he was *friends* with her brother. How had this happened?

Marcus looked delighted by Zoey's puzzled expression. "Cody's one of the judges at camp," he explained. "He came up to us after we played today and told us how much he liked our T-shirts. So I said my sister made them, and that you had a blog et cetera, and then *he* asked *me* if you were Sew Zoey!"

Zoey couldn't believe her ears. How in the world did *Cody Calloway* know about her blog?

Cody grinned. "See, this is my little sister, Dakota. She's your age, and she's a huge fan! And I knew she'd love to meet you, and, uh, well . . ." Cody paused, looking embarrassed.

Marcus filled in the rest. "And *I* said *you'd* love to meet Cody. So I texted Dad about inviting them over, and he said he'd make fajitas!"

Zoey couldn't believe her ears. She knew she was in the middle of probably one of the most exciting moments of her life, and all she wanted to do was hug her brother and tell him how awesome he was for bringing Cody Calloway to her house, even though at the same time she was *mortified* that Cody obviously knew she had a huge crush on him.

"I love fajitas," Zoey squeaked. She took a deep breath so she wouldn't faint.

Nervously, Dakota stepped forward to shake Zoey's hand also. "I'm so thrilled to meet you," she said. "I love your blog and your Etsy site. I buy all of your stuff!"

Suddenly, the name clicked. *Dakota.* "Wait, are you *Dakota Brown*?" Zoey asked. "You're my biggest fan!"

Dakota nodded, pleased that Zoey knew her. "That's me!"

Zoey looked from Dakota to Cody and back. She noticed Dakota had the same thick dirty blond hair as Cody, though hers hung well below her shoulders. She also had the same dark eyebrows as her brother. "But why do you guys have different last names?"

Cody shrugged. "My name is really Cody Brown, but my parents and the record label decided I should use a stage name, so I can still have some anonymity, because I started so young. Calloway is my mom's maiden name, so I use that."

"Oh right," Zoey said. "That makes perfect sense." She looked from Cody to Dakota to Cody again. She couldn't believe both her music star crush and biggest fan were standing in front of her *and* were brother and sister!

"Come in!" Zoey said quickly. "I can't believe we're still standing in the front door. I'm so sorry. This is just, well, very, very exciting!"

Mr. Webber came up to the door to meet everyone and then ushered them into the kitchen to sit down. He'd put guacamole and chips and sodas on the table, so they could munch on something while Mr. Webber finished making the fajitas.

"I like that you eat in your kitchen," Cody said. "My mom always makes us have family dinners in the dining room! It's too stuffy, I think."

Mr. Webber laughed. "Zoey uses the dining room as her office, and we've all gotten so used to it, we don't even think about it anymore!"

The whole group laughed and started in on the snacks. Zoey really couldn't believe she was sitting at her own kitchen table, eating chips with Cody Calloway. What would she tell her friends?

"So, Zoey," Cody said. "I mean, *Sew Zoey*. Do you think you could make a shirt like Marcus's for me?"

Zoey nearly passed out. Make a shirt for Cody? Was he serious? She'd make him a thousand!

"Well, sure," she managed to answer, almost calmly. "What do you want it to look like?"

Cody described it, using his band's logo as the basis and offering to sketch it out for her. Zoey told him that wouldn't be necessary; she knew it by heart. He laughed and gently punched her on the shoulder, which helped to put her at ease. Cody may have been a superstar, but underneath he was just a boy, like her brother, who liked fajitas and music and cool T-shirts.

"I'll start on the shirt right away," she promised him. "But how can I send it to you?"

"That's easy," Dakota said. "Just bring it to the concert on Sunday and give it to him then." Then she slapped her hand over her mouth, and looked guiltily at her brother. "Oh my gosh, Cody!" she gushed. "I'm so sorry! They didn't know you're the guest performer!"

Cody rolled his eyes and groaned. "They didn't until *now*, no. Thanks, Dakota."

Zoey couldn't believe it. Cody would be performing at the rock camp's final concert! She would actually get to see him play again!

"Please don't tell anyone," Cody said. "It's supposed to be a secret, but my sister isn't so good with secrets. . . . And please don't tell anyone we were here tonight for dinner, either. If word gets out, then people might guess about the concert, and the promoters will get really upset."

"Of course we won't," Marcus assured him. "We won't tell anyone."

Zoey nodded fervently, pledging her silence, but on the inside, she felt like she might burst with the news. The biggest thing that had ever happened to her in her whole life, and she couldn't tell her best friends. It would be torture!

Cody nudged Dakota with his shoulder. "Little sisters—you can't take 'em anywhere," he joked.

"That's for sure," Marcus agreed. Then he gestured at the T-shirt Zoey had made for him. "But they're all right sometimes."

Zoey thought about Sophie and Libby and how much Libby loved Sophie, even though Sophie drove her nuts. Zoey wondered if she drove Marcus nuts the same way. Probably. But one thing was for sure, they all loved each other. And that mattered much, much more.

After all, it was Zoey's older brother who had delivered Cody Calloway to her very own kitchen. If that wasn't love, what was?

CHAPTER 11

No One Will EVER Believe Me . . .

OMG! I met a very famous "someone" the other day, AND also met one of my biggest Sew Zoey supporters, but I'm SWORN to secrecy and can't say who they are. It's pretty much rocked my world! (That's a clue, but I can't tell you why!) So I guess I need to stop blogging about it. But I'll just say this: WOW.

This week I'm finally finishing up my very first interior design project (Priti's new bedroom), and my outfit for Sophie, AND the band T-shirts for Marcus are done. So what on Earth will I do with all my time? Oh, that's right—school starts soon! I guess I'll be doing homework. And speaking of homework . . . What do you think of this sketch for a possible first-day-of-school outfit? Is the belt too much?

Nah, I didn't think so, either! Good minds think alike!

Finally, it was time to set up Priti's new room. Mr. Holbrooke had been secretly assembling the new furniture while Priti was at her mother's house, and Zoey and Aunt Lulu were headed over to his apartment with all of the accessories, pillows, pictures, and duvet. When they were done, it would be perfectly Priti!

They spent the morning arranging and rear-ranging every piece until Lulu and Zoey both felt it was perfect. Zoey didn't want to let down her best friend. When the room was finally ready, Mr.

Holbrooke called Mrs. Holbrooke and told her to bring Priti over.

Priti arrived and insisted on being blindfolded. When Zoey guided her into the room and removed the blindfold, Priti covered her mouth with both hands and shrieked.

"I can't *believe* it!" she said. "It's the most beautiful room I've ever, ever, *ever* seen!"

She walked around the room in a circle, stopping to admire each piece, from the night table to the pillows, to the framed pictures of her and her sisters and friends on the walls. Zoey had hand painted a frame with a picture of her, Priti, Kate, and Libby, and Priti touched it lovingly with one finger.

"I can hardly believe I get to *sleep* here! And hang out! And do homework!" She looked at her dad. "And all the new furniture, Dad! *Thank* you!"

Mr. Holbrooke looked delighted by Priti's reaction. It was obvious how much he wanted her to be happy.

Then, out of nowhere, Priti's eyes filled up with tears. Sad tears. And she started to cry.

"I'm sorry everyone," she said. "It's just . . . this is

my dream room, but the *situation* is not so dreamy."

Mr. Holbrooke rushed over to his daughter and hugged her tight. Aunt Lulu and Zoey looked on sympathetically.

"I love you, honey, and I know this isn't easy," Mr. Holbrooke said. "I don't expect a pretty bedroom to suddenly make it okay that your mother and I have separated. I just wanted to make the best of a tough situation and to give you a space you'll be happy to come to when you're here with me. I'm still getting used to calling this place 'home' too, you know!"

Priti hugged her father back, hard. "Thank you for saying that. And thank you for this amazing room! I know it's going to get easier. And I really do love it."

Aunt Lulu and Zoey took turns giving Priti hugs too. Zoey kept an arm around her friend and said, "You know, everyone thinks families have to look a certain way to be 'happy,' but that's not really true. After all, Lulu's my aunt, but in a lot of ways, she's like my surrogate mom. Maybe it's not normal for everyone, but it works for us!"

Priti nodded and smiled, her tears quickly drying up. "You're right, Zoey. I wouldn't trade my mom and dad for anyone else's in the world, even if we're not all in the same place anymore."

After hanging out with the Holbrookes for a while, Aunt Lulu dropped Zoey off at home. Zoey was eating lunch when she heard her phone ding, and checked it, to see if it was a message from Priti.

It wasn't. It was from Daphne Shaw.

Zoey's heart started pounding as she opened the e-mail and began to read.

Dear Zoey,

Hello! I've just returned from two weeks in Italy, where I was sourcing fabrics for my line. Imagine my surprise when I finally reached the bottom of my snail mail pile this morning and found your letter! It had been sitting here waiting for me all this time. Yes, I am Fashionsista! I use my real name online for business, and different pseudonyms for personal things. Also, I confess, while I really enjoyed being your secret fashion "fairy godmother" for a while, I'm glad that you now know it's me. I even thought about telling you when you came to visit in June, but I just wasn't ready to let go of my fun little secret. ☺ Maybe one day you'll return the favor to another talented young designer!

Xoxo, Daphne

Zoey swallowed hard. It was true. Daphne Shaw was Fashionsista! It was both wonderful and a bit sad to finally know the truth for sure. The mystery had been *such* fun. But Daphne was right—maybe it would be Zoey's turn next to be someone else's fashion fairy godmother! And in the meantime, Zoey had to think of just the right way to say thank you to Daphne for all the support and inspiration she'd given her. She vowed to make the perfect thank-you gift.

On Saturday Mr. Webber dropped Zoey and one very carefully ironed dress off at the Flynn house. Zoey had worked extra hard to make every last stitch perfect, and she couldn't wait for Sophie to try on the finished product.

As Mrs. Flynn helped Sophie into the dress, Zoey couldn't help feeling nervous. Would Sophie love it?

Luckily, Sophie was beaming from the moment she saw it. Then she tried it on. She looked at herself in the mirror and did twirl after twirl.

"It fits her perfectly!" Mrs. Flynn exclaimed. "Thank you, Zoey. I can't believe how darling it turned out. I know she's going to wear it all the time."

Zoey smiled, relieved. "Great—I'm so glad to hear it. And I've got a little surprise for you as well. . . ." Zoey reached into her bag and pulled out carefully folded extra bands of fabric in varying patterns to zip on to the bottom of the dress.

Sophie walked over to Zoey, and Zoey demonstrated how easily Mrs. Flynn could zip on an extra few inches of fabric whenever the dress started looking a little short.

"See?" said Zoey. "The zipper is hidden underneath, so you won't see that it's not part of the original dress! Hopefully, this will be one outfit she won't outgrow in the next five minutes!"

Mrs. Flynn looked absolutely bowled over. She threw her arms around Zoey and hugged her tight. "You're a *real* designer, Miss Zoey. Only you could have come up with something so perfect for my Sophie! We just love it. Thank you, thank you!"

Zoey beamed, almost as brightly as Sophie.

Then Sophie turned to her and said, "You're the best, Zoey! And I have a surprise for *you*, too! Come up to my room, okay?"

Zoey looked at Mrs. Flynn, who shrugged and didn't seem to know what Sophie meant either. They both followed Sophie up to her bedroom and watched as she stood beside her dollhouse, which was covered with a sheet.

"Surprise!" Sophie yelled, yanking the sheet off the dollhouse and pointing to it. "I made a creative project out of swatches too, just like you and your aunt!"

Confused, Zoey squinted at the dollhouse. She couldn't believe what she saw. In its dining room was a chandelier made from the dangly earring Mrs. Flynn couldn't find the other day. One of Zoey's mirrored buttons hung on the wall like a real mirror, and a round rug in the little living room was clearly the swatch that had been cut out of Aunt Lulu's fabric book! There was a pillow swatch used as a comforter, and in that same bedroom Zoey's missing ribbon had been cut in half and tacked up one either side of the window like drapes. Zoey saw missing piece after missing piece from her sewing supplies, all repurposed in Sophie's dollhouse!

"What do you think?" Sophie asked, bursting with pride.

Zoey was flabbergasted. She didn't know what to say. Zoey *did* have a fashion burglar, but she was only six years old!

Mrs. Flynn's face was a bright, tomato red. "Sophie Flynn! Did you *take* all those things? That's *stealing*!"

Sophie immediately looked panicked, not to mention disappointed that no one was telling her how beautiful her "project" was.

"I didn't steal anything!" Sophie protested. "Zoey said swatches are free for people who are designing houses and clothes! And that's what I did! It's just that mine is a dollhouse and not a real house."

"Oh, Sophie, you misunderstood, honey," Mrs. Flynn said, still obviously embarrassed. "Those things all *belonged* to Zoey and her aunt. Except for the earring—that was mine. And you didn't ask any of us first—which is what you should do next time, okay?"

Zoey was trying very hard not to burst out laughing. Sophie had been wrong to do what she did, but Zoey completely understood how Sophie had *misunderstood* the rules about swatches. She'd thought she was designing! And in light of what Daphne Shaw had said to Zoey about being a mentor to another future designer, Zoey didn't want to say anything to crush Sophie's budding talent.

"You know Sophie, you really did a great job," Zoey said. "You chose beautiful colors, and I love the way you arranged everything. You might really have a future in design!"

Sophie seemed to grow taller with each word of praise.

"Maybe you should take a sewing class or an art class," Zoey suggested gently. "And I'm sure Aunt Lulu would be happy to give you some old fabric books to use for your dollhouse interior designs."

Mrs. Flynn looked incredibly grateful to Zoey for her kind words. "We can definitely sign you up for some art classes," she said to Sophie. "But there will be absolutely no more taking things without asking!"

Sophie quickly agreed. "Okay. I didn't mean to, anyway. I just love beautiful things. . . ."

Zoey smiled and gave Sophie a warm hug. She understood perfectly, because she too loved beautiful things. Including Sophie Flynn.

When Zoey got home, still laughing to herself about her missing button hanging as a mirror over the "fireplace" in Sophie's dollhouse, she saw a package on her doorstep. It was from Daphne Shaw, and it was large. She quickly ripped it open, excited to see what her not-so-secret mentor was now sending her.

It was a bolt of personalized fabric, printed with some of Zoey's sketches! Daphne included a note that explained how she'd had the fabric made in one of the mills in Italy while she was there, using the sketches from Zoey's blog. Zoey truly couldn't believe it. The different sketches, all in black and white, made a beautiful graphic print, and she couldn't wait to put the fabric to good use and create something amazing with it!

Zoey unfolded a yard of the fabric, running her fingertips over her own sketches, rendered so beautifully on the cloth. She thought about Priti, and how down she'd been lately about her parents splitting up, and how Zoey herself could feel down sometimes about her mother not being with her anymore. But over the years Zoey had learned how lucky she really was and that it wasn't worth focusing on the person she *didn't* have around, because the people she *did* have were all so wonderful! She knew it wasn't something Priti could learn overnight, but Zoey would be there to help her every step of the way. And in the meantime, the fabric from Daphne Shaw gave Zoey an idea for something nice she could do for each of her friends, including her new ones—Sophie and Dakota—to remind them all how lucky they were to have one another.

----------CHAPTER 12 ----------

Sayonara, Summer!

I can't believe it's really the end of summer, and we get to celebrate it by going to my brother's camp concert with a special guest band! (Not that I have ANY idea who that might be . . . none at all ☺). What a summer this has been—a trip to New York, sleepaway camp, my first interior design project, learning to screen print, the unveiling of Fashionsista. Yes, that's right! My fairy godmother has *finally* confirmed her identity! I've decided not to announce her name publicly and to just keep the secret between the two of us. It seems more special that way. But I would like to say publicly (bloggingly?), THANK YOU, FASHIONSISTA, for the many wonderful things you have done for me!

Here's a sketch of something I'm currently working on as a surprise gift for someone. It's a circle skirt, with plenty of flounce to it, and it wraps around the waist, so it's totally adjustable. This is very important, since I can't exactly ask for measurements from someone I'm planning to surprise! What's really going to make it pop is the fabric I plan to use (it's not actually a floral print) . . . and that shall remain a secret for now! SEW LONG!

Zoey couldn't believe it—she really, really couldn't. She was at the Camp of Rock's big finale concert at the beach, and her brother's band had just played (looking extremely cool in their T-shirts from Zoey and leather cuffs from Allie), and she was surrounded by practically everyone she knew. Her dad, Aunt Lulu and her boyfriend, Zoey's three best friends, along with Mrs. Flynn and Sophie. Zoey had even seen her friend Gabe in the crowd. It seemed like everyone had turned out for the concert to find out who the special guest act would be.

The bands from camp had all played, and there was a brief intermission while the crew set up for the main event. Zoey's dad had offered to go get everyone sodas, and Zoey was happily catching up with Kate, Libby, and Priti, when out of nowhere, Shannon came up to them.

Priti looked at Shannon suspiciously, as if she were unsure of what she might say, but Zoey greeted Shannon warmly. After all, she had helped Zoey finish the shirts for the band. Without Shannon, they wouldn't have gotten done!

"Hi, everyone," Shannon said tentatively. "I don't mean to interrupt. . . . I just wanted to tell Zoey something."

Zoey could sense Shannon was nervous without Ivy and Bree by her side. Zoey nodded at her encouragingly. "Sure, what is it?"

Shannon smiled. "I just wanted to say how amazing your brother's band looks in their shirts. You did a great job. And they sounded awesome too!"

Zoey nearly gawked at all the compliments coming out of Shannon's mouth, but quickly covered up her surprise. Shannon had been nice to her, and she deserved the same in return. Maybe she really was changing for the better.

"Thank you!" Zoey said. "And you deserve credit too. I'd never have been able to get the shirts done as quickly as I did without your screen-printing expertise."

Shannon grinned, pleased. "Oh, well, sure. It was no problem. I've got to go—I just wanted to say hi. Bye, everybody."

Zoey nodded, and her friends all managed to say good-bye without sounding too astonished.

"I never thought I'd see the day," Priti remarked. "But Shannon actually seemed nice!"

"If she could just stay away from Ivy and Bree, I bet she *could* be nice," Kate agreed. "Maybe this year will be different! I wouldn't mind that at all."

"Me neither," said Libby, who'd often been

teased by Ivy about her height. "One less mean girl in the world is something to celebrate."

The girls couldn't finish their conversation, because just then, the lights dimmed and the crowd started clapped and yelling wildly, even though they still didn't know who the secret performer was.

Zoey giggled to herself, trying to contain her excitement at seeing Cody sing again, but this time as his sort-of friend!

Cody strode out to the middle of the stage, and all at once, hundreds of girls screamed, "IT'S CODY CALLOWAY!"

Zoey and her friends yelled and cheered and jumped up and down. Zoey was just as excited as everyone else—and it was because Cody was *wearing* the T-shirt Zoey had made for him! She'd given it to Marcus that morning to deliver, and Cody must have liked it so much, he put it on right away! Zoey felt like she'd died and gone to heaven. There was Cody Calloway, onstage in front of hundreds of fans, wearing a *Sew Zoey* design! None of her friends recognized the shirt as Zoey's, because it was screen printed and based on Cody's band's logo.

The girls watched the concert, enjoying every minute of Cody's set. Zoey felt like she was on the moon, she was so happy!

As soon as the band finished, and Zoey and her friends had clapped so hard their hands were hurting, they started to head toward the door that led to the backstage area, where they were joined by Sophie and Mrs. Flynn.

Sophie ran to Zoey and hugged her. "Zoey, did you see the shirt Cody was wearing? It looked just like the ones you made for your brother's band!"

Libby immediately squeezed Sophie's shoulder and shushed her. "It's just a coincidence, Sophie," she said.

Before Zoey could say anything, Cody and his sister, Dakota, came through the door from backstage and were standing directly in front of them. Zoey's friends all gasped, completely overwhelmed that they were standing *two feet away* from Cody Calloway. Dakota was wearing all Sew Zoey clothing, and Cody was still wearing his T-shirt. Priti swooned from the shock of being so close to him and started to lose her balance. Kate, still athletic, even with a sling on, caught Priti with her good arm and helped her upright again. Libby's face was shockingly pink.

Cody came even closer to Zoey and touched her arm. "Thanks so much for the shirt, Zoey," he said. "It turned out amazing! I might order a few more from you!"

Libby, still bright pink and overwhelmed, spat out, "You *know* Cody Calloway? You *made him a shirt*?"

Priti started to swoon again, but luckily, Kate was still standing beside her and kept her from falling.

Zoey nodded, thrilled and relieved to finally be able to spill the beans to her friends. "Yes! And this is his sister, Dakota. Believe me, it's been the hardest secret I've ever kept. Marcus brought Cody and Dakota over last week, and Dakota knew all about Sew Zoey and buys a lot of my clothes! Isn't that funny?"

"So I *was* right!" Sophie piped up. "Zoey *did* make that shirt!"

Libby looked embarrassed at having shushed Sophie earlier. "Sorry, Soph," she said. "I guess I need to start listening to you more often. You have a real fashion eye, kid!"

Sophie grinned, and everyone introduced themselves. Then, out of nowhere, a flock of photographers spotted Cody and started to push toward them. Before Cody and Dakota left with their security team, Cody whispered to Zoey, "Marcus invited us back to your house for dinner again. We'll see you there!"

Before Zoey could respond, he and Dakota were gone, and she was standing with her baffled friends, all of whom looked like they might pass out. Even Kate, who didn't really care much about Cody Calloway, was shaking a little.

"Start talking, Webber," Priti ordered. "You've got a *lot* to explain."

"So do *you*, Holbrooke," said Kate to Priti. "You're always saying Cody Calloway isn't all that, and then as soon as we see him, you're falling all over the place!"

Priti's cheeks flamed red. "Well, fine, maybe he has a *little* more star power than I originally thought. He's still no Joey Joseph-Brown. But I'll have dinner with him at your house, Zoey. That's for sure."

To Zoey's delight, Mr. Webber had invited *everyone* back to their house, and ordered fifteen large pizzas and several big salads. Marcus and Cody were in the basement with Marcus's bandmates, while Cody's parents were in the kitchen with Mr. Webber, Aunt Lulu, John, and Mrs. Flynn. Zoey seized the opportunity to run up to her room and retrieve the special gifts she'd made for her friends, Allie, Sophie, and Dakota, who were all hanging out in the living room with Sophie, who never stopped smiling and looked absolutely delighted to be included.

Zoey came downstairs and distributed the wrapped gifts. She'd gone back to screen-printing class at the end of the week and had her screen-printing teacher help her stretch the fabric Fashionsista had given her onto mini–stretch boards, turning each sketch into a piece of wall art for the girls' rooms. Each piece of art was centered on an outfit Zoey had sketched for one of her friends.

For Allie, it was some of the accessories from the Etsy shop. For Dakota, a sketch of one of the shirts she'd bought. For Sophie, whose sketch had been finalized too late to be on the fabric, Zoey had made a piece of wall art using the sketch from the Libby dress she'd made Libby, and then a second, miniature version for her dollhouse! Zoey knew that Sophie tended to like anything her big sister liked, and wanted to be just like Libby, so she thought that would be the right choice for her. And the dollhouse mini seemed fitting as well.

Everyone *loved* the gifts, and Zoey was relieved when Allie gave her an extra-long hug, and whispered, "Thanks, Zoey—you're a good friend."

Zoey felt certain then that Allie had forgiven her for the mix-up with the gifts for the band. Zoey sighed with happiness. She loved giving gifts, and giving handmade, personal gifts was the very best!

Dakota, whose ready smile and quick wit was helping her make fast friends with everyone in the group, vowed she was even *more* of a Sew Zoey fan, if that was possible.

"These are beautiful, Zoey," Dakota said. "And I

love that you picked a part of the fabric with that blouse of yours I ordered. I wear it all the time!"

"What else are you going to do with all this beautiful fabric Fashionsista made for you?" Kate asked.

"Well, I made one more gift with it," Zoey told everyone. "A skirt for Fashionsista. It felt too strange for me to wear fabric with my *own* sketches on it, but I thought she might like to wear it, knowing what an inspiration she's been to me!"

"You're *my* inspiration," Sophie piped up, and for once, Libby didn't look annoyed by Sophie, but instead gave her a proud half hug.

"Mine, too," Dakota agreed. Then, flipping her long dirty blond hair over her shoulder and looking around at everyone gathered in Zoey's living room, she said, "I can't believe you all get to be *friends* with Sew Zoey! Do you know how amazing that is?"

Priti laughed, almost hysterically. "Do *you* know how amazing it is that you're Cody Calloway's sister?"

Then they all laughed together, and Zoey felt like she was, in fact, the luckiest girl in the entire world. She realized she didn't have to sell a bazillion pieces online to be successful—she was *already* successful! Because success, to her, was having fun and learning and trying new things. It was more than enough to have a wonderful fan like Dakota, a wonderful mentor like Daphne Shaw, and a wonderful group of friends to celebrate with. She had plenty of time to grow her business.

The pizzas arrived, and everyone sat down together to eat. It was truly an amazing end to an amazing summer. With a brand-new school year just around the corner, Zoey wondered if things could possibly get better than they were right then. She felt like she had seen a snippet of a beautiful piece of material . . .

And she couldn't wait to see the rest of it!

Watch out for
more swatches . . .
Turn the page for a
sneak peek at the next book
in the Sew Zoey series:

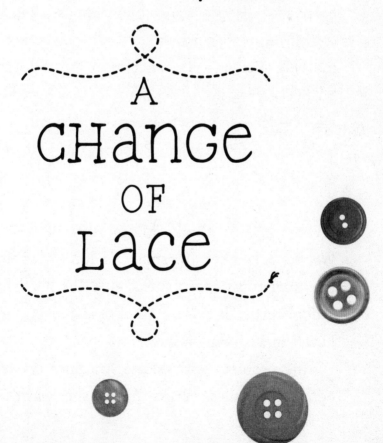

A
CHANGE
OF
LACE

The Long and the Short of It

Can you believe school starts next week?! Summer vacation always seems so long at the beginning, and then, at the end, it seems like it flashed by in an instant. All of a sudden it's about to be over, as if time magically starts to speed up in August.

It's been a really fun summer, getting to visit Daphne Shaw's studio, going to sleepaway camp for the first time, and taking a screen-printing class, but there's something exciting about starting a new school year, too. I'm designing a new outfit for the first day of school, but I'm keeping that under wraps for now. Instead, here are "the long and short of it" skirts inspired by how I feel about time this summer. I hope you like them!

"What do you think, Marie Antoinette?" Zoey Webber asked her dressmaker's dummy as she put the final touches on the sketch for her back-to-school outfit. "Is this a winner or is it just . . . weird? I can't make up my mind."

The problem with Marie Antoinette was that being a headless dress form, she wasn't very forthcoming with her opinion.

Zoey sighed and looked at the pictures she'd printed out after watching a movie from the 1960s. They were of an Italian actress wearing a wide-legged halter-top jumpsuit. Zoey'd thought it was such a cool and different look, perfect for her to update with Zoey magic. But now, comparing the sixties outfit to her sketch, she wasn't so sure.

Just then the doorbell rang, interrupting her musings.

"Hey, Zo! The Holbrookes are here!" her brother, Marcus, announced from the bottom of the stairs.

Zoey slipped on her flip-flops, grabbed her purse and cell phone, and ran downstairs. She had a mall date with one of her best friends, Priti, to help her shop for a new back-to-school outfit.

"See you later, Marcus!" she called on the way out the door.

Zoey slid into the backseat next to Priti. "I can't believe school starts next week," she said. "I'm excited, but still I'm not sure if I'm ready."

"This summer has gone by so quickly," Mrs. Holbrooke said. "It seems like only yesterday you girls got out of school. A lot has happened since then, hasn't it?"

"You can say that again," Priti said with a sigh. She was still adjusting to the idea that her parents were getting a divorce and to the fact that her dad had moved out of the family home.

Mrs. Holbrooke gave Priti a worried look in the rearview mirror, which transformed into a cheerful smile the minute she caught Zoey's eye.

"Well, you'll have to pick out a great outfit to wow everyone on the first day, right, Priti?"

"Uh-huh. Sure," Priti agreed without any of her normal bounce and enthusiasm.

Zoey wondered what was going on—had Priti and her mom had a fight before she had gotten into the car?

She spent the rest of the ride to the mall describing how she came up with the idea for her back-to-school outfit and asking Priti and Mrs. Holbrooke what they thought about the idea.

"I think it sounds fab," Priti said. "Why are you worrying so much, Zo? Weren't you voted Best Dressed last year?"

"That just means I have more of a reputation to keep up!" Zoey said.

Mrs. Holbrooke pulled up outside the mall.

"I'm sure you'll look adorable, Zoey. You always do," she said. "I'll see you in a few hours. And you know the rules. . . . Don't talk to strangers and call if you're even going to be a minute late for pick-up time."

As she drove off, Priti dragged Zoey toward the mall doors. "Come on! Let's shop till we drop!"

The girls browsed a few of the popular chain stores before ending up at their favorite clothing shop, My Best Friend's Closet. While Priti browsed, Zoey picked out a few outfits she knew her friend would love—colorful clothes, sparkly accessories, an adorable belt with a fake jeweled buckle.

She walked over to the display rack where Priti was standing.

"What do you think?" she said, holding up the clothes she'd picked out. "Perfect, right? Do you want to try them on?"

"Sure," Priti said, taking the clothes from her.

But Zoey noticed that before she walked to

the dressing room to try them on, Priti grabbed a bunch of black clothes off a rack where she must have placed them while she'd been browsing.

That's odd, Zoey thought. Her friend was usually the queen of bright colors.

Priti came out wearing the first of the outfits Zoey'd picked out for her.

"It looks awesome!" Zoey said.

Priti looked at her reflection in the mirror.

"I don't know. I'm not . . ." She paused, turning to look at it from another angle. "Let me try on the other one."

Zoey waited, wondering what Priti didn't like about the first outfit, which looked really good on her.

The second outfit looked even better on Priti than the first.

"What do you think?" Zoey asked.

"It's cute," Priti said. "I like it."

"Great!" Zoey said. "Just in time, because I'm getting hungry."

"I just want to try one more thing," Priti said. "I'll meet you by the register."

When Priti went to the register to pay, all the clothes she was carrying were completely . . . black.

Zoey was surprised, because wearing all one color—particularly a dark color like black—was so unlike her friend's usual style. Seeing a striped scarf hanging nearby, she took it from the display and draped it around Priti's neck.

"What do you think? It would brighten up your outfit a little."

Priti shrugged and removed the scarf from around her neck, placing it back on the display.

"It's nice, but I'm good without it."

"What about the jeweled belt?" Zoey suggested.

"No, it's okay. I'm just going to buy the jeans and the shirt."

As Priti paid for her purchases, Zoey wondered what was going on with her friend. Maybe Priti wanted to experiment with her style, and there definitely was nothing wrong with that. Zoey was all about being adventurous with clothes.

It was just . . . Going from glitzy to goth seemed pretty *dramatic*. On the other hand, Zoey thought, Priti had always had a flair for the dramatic. . . .

CHLOE TAYLOR

learned to sew when she was a little girl. She loved watching her grandmother Louise turn a scrap of blue fabric into a simple-but-fabulous dress, nightgown, or even a bathing suit in an instant. It was magical! Now that she's grown up, she still loves fashion: it's like art that you can wear. This is her first middle grade series. She lives, writes, and window-shops in New York City.

NANCY ZHANG

is an illustrator and an art and fashion lover with a passion for all beautiful things. She has published her work in the art books *L'Oiseau Rouge* and *Street Impressions* and in various fashion magazines and on websites. Visit her at her blog: www.xiaoxizhang.com. She currently lives in Berlin, Germany.

Great stories are like great accessories: You can never have too many! Collect all the books in the Sew Zoey series:

Ready to Wear

On Pins and Needles

Lights, Camera, Fashion!

Stitches and Stones

Cute as a Button

A Tangled Thread

Knot Too Shabby!

Swatch Out!